Behind Closed Doors

Behind Closed Doors

MIRIAM HALAHMY

Holiday House / New York

HOLIDAY HOUSE is registered in the U.S. Patent and Trademark Office.
Printed and Bound in March 2017 at Maple Press, York, PA, USA.
www.holidayhouse.com
First Edition
1 3 5 7 9 10 8 6 4 2

Library of Congress Cataloging-in-Publication Data

Names: Halahmy, Miriam, author.
Title: Behind closed doors / by Miriam Halahmy.
Description: First edition. | New York : Holiday House, [2016] | Summary:
In alternating chapters, teens Tasha and Josie tell how each becomes
temporarily homeless and how they find strength and friendship together as
they try to regain control of their lives.
Identifiers: LCCN 2015040847 | ISBN 9780823436415 (hardcover)
Subjects: | CYAC: Homeless persons—Fiction. | Family problems—Fiction. |
Mothers and daughters—Fiction. | Dating (Social customs)—Fiction. |
Friendship—Fiction.
Classification: LCC PZ7.H12825 Beh 2016 | DDC [Fic]—dc23 LC record available at
https://lccn.loc.gov/2015040847

For all homeless young people who have
no safe place to sleep tonight

Home! Home! sweet, sweet home!
There's no place like home!

John Howard Payne, "Home, Sweet Home," 1827

Home is where we start from.

T. S. Eliot, *Four Quartets,* "East Coker"

Behind Closed Doors

1. Josie

"Until I was ten years old, I thought everyone had Christmas in the bedroom."

Shrieks all down the line at the bus stop.

Oh God!

I pull my earphones out. I've done it again. Spoken out loud when I'm listening to music. But everyone's been talking about Christmas, and it's only the first week in October. They're driving me crazy.

"The bedroom?" says Tasha Brown, not looking up from her phone. "Like, how crazy weird is that?"

I duck my head and look around for the bus as I flush right down my neck.

"Sounds cool," says Dom, with his kind smile. "My little brothers would kill to have a tree in the bedroom."

He's Tasha's friend. "Sweet little Dom," she calls him, which is a bit patronizing.

"Yeah, right," says Tasha in a bored voice. "They can electrocute themselves on the fairy lights. Very cool."

She still doesn't look up from her phone. Tasha manages to look goth even in uniform. It's the black tights with laced boots and short skirt.

My uniform's recycled. Mum's a collector, and she's saving the planet.

"We're having Christmas in Spain this year," says someone, and the chatter turns to high-top bikinis.

I put my earphones back in and try to look as though I'm listening to music, but I can still hear Tasha's bored voice. "The only good thing about Christmas is the cash."

She's not even looking at her sweet little Dom, but he grins and nods, his head bobbing up and down like an eager puppy. They're a strange pair, I can't help thinking, but I still wish I was part of the crowd instead of being out on the edge all the time.

What do you expect, Josie Tate, when you say stuff like having Christmas in the bedroom? I feel myself shudder. I hate anyone knowing our private business.

The bus to the swimming pool arrives, and I make my escape. Everyone else takes the other bus to the shops. I'm so desperate for a shower. No hot water in the phys ed block all week, and I haven't washed my hair since Monday. They built the new pool two years ago, miles away on the edge of town, and the showers are exactly the kind I want in my own flat one day: high pressure, constant hot water.

By the time I've showered and dressed, it's so late that I don't even dry my hair. I push all my stuff into my backpack and hurry out into the corridor. But my hair's dripping in my eyes and I bump into someone. My backpack spills all over the floor, and I'm down on my knees grabbing my underpants, the polka dot ones. Can today get any more embarrassing?

"Here, let me help."

Looking up, I see a boy bending down, tanned skin, very long arms—and he's naked!

"Cover up," I hiss, but I don't think he heard me. What if he saw my underwear? But why would he care? He's not wearing *anything.*

I'm trying to push my hair out of my eyes and repack my stuff. When I look up again the boy's stood up, and he's wearing a pair of black Speedos. Relief whooshes through me.

"Your toothpaste?" he says, holding it out in his right hand.

He's so tall—must be at least six feet—but he's lean with such long legs and arms. His nails are perfectly scrubbed, white half-moons gleaming against golden skin, and he has these amazing almond-shaped eyes.

"Thanks," I say, getting up and taking the squashed tube. I stuff it into my pack.

A noise starts up at the end of the corridor. A couple of girls are coming toward us with long, slender bodies and black suits, and I can see the word *Torpedoes* emblazoned in silver over the hip.

"Coming?" says one of the girls, a blond ponytail swinging over her shoulder.

"Not right now, uh, Chantelle," says the boy, and for some reason I feel another little whoosh of relief.

Chantelle shrugs and walks on with her friends. The boy turns back to me and says, "I was going to the canteen before my next swim. You wanna get some coffee?"

"I can't," I say. "I'm late."

"Oh."

There's something about the way his mouth settles in a line that's familiar. Relief, I think, looking at the long thin line of his eyes. They've retreated into the sockets, almost disappearing.

And then I realize. He's lonely, like me, and I almost decide to skip my paper route. Only Friday's payday, and I need the money.

"I'm a working girl," I say with a grin.

"Oh sure," he says, his arms hanging loose at his sides.

We stand there for a minute in silence, and I'm about to go when the boy says, "Maybe we could have a swim sometime. I'm here every morning."

I open my mouth to say I can't swim and don't even own a suit. Then I shut it again. "Every morning?" I say.

"Sure. How about tomorrow?"

"Sure," I say.

His body shifts slightly as if he's pleased and I walk off, a grin spreading across my face.

All the way back on the bus I try out the word *sure* in my mouth. The boy has an American accent and *sure* is an American word, isn't it? It's such a strong, confident word, so much better than *okay,* or *all right,* or *maybe,* or any of the other things he might have said.

My paper route flies by as I call out "Sure!" to customers on their doorsteps. By six thirty I'm finished, and I take my pay packet to Terry's Café. My routine's always the same: a mug of tea, then check my pay and split it into three piles—expenses, school stuff, savings.

I'm saving for my own flat. That'd show Tasha Brown, I think, scooping the money up.

I want a studio, which means one bedroom, a kitchen/living room and a bathroom. I need £500.00 for a deposit. I've saved £35.50, so it's a long-term plan. I want my own high-pressure hot shower and my own toilet.

Then as I walk home I start wondering which school swim boy goes to. He's older than me, maybe eighteen. He could be at college. How can someone so gorgeous and with such a lovely, deep American voice and almond-shaped eyes possibly be lonely? He must have hundreds of friends and loads of girlfriends. That Chantelle looked like a model.

He's not lonely; you're mad, Josie Tate, I tell myself as I turn onto my street.

A couple is lingering right outside our front door. We don't have a front garden, and we never open the door when anyone's around. Now I'll have to wait until they move on. I look at my watch and walk past, glaring at them, but they don't seem to notice.

Then the woman calls out, "Pick me up by nine."

"Fine," says the man, and he grabs her again for a totally long kiss. They're practically leaning against our door.

Finally, they walk off in opposite directions. I take out my key, turn it in the lock, squeeze through the tiny space and kick the door shut behind me.

"Mum?" I call out.

"Up here."

I turn sideways and shuffle down the narrow space in the hall, taking care not to tip the boxes at the far end that loom toward me like badly stacked bricks. But when I get to the stairs, they've almost disappeared since this morning.

"What's happened?" I call out.

"Just sorting. Mind the stairs."

"What do you think I'm doing?" I mutter as I haul myself over the first two steps and clamber to the top floor.

The landing's stacked to the ceiling with newspapers, boxes, piles of clothes, plastic bottles and cans. The bathroom door's jammed permanently open, the tub full to the brim with more stuff and so many sacks and boxes on the floor that half the sink's covered. You have to put your feet on a bulging black sack to sit on the toilet.

So nothing's changed up here, I tell myself with relief.

I put my head around Mum's door. "Sorting what?"

"Socks and plastic bottles."

Mum's sitting cross-legged on the bed, piles of socks and squashed bottles over the half of the duvet that isn't piled with bags. She was laid off from her office job months ago and wants to work in a recycling center, but nothing's come up.

"My severance pay will last ages, Josie, so don't worry," she keeps telling me.

She helps out in secondhand shops Monday to Thursday and doesn't really bother to get dressed on Fridays, just lounges around in baggy tracksuit bottoms and the same sweatshirt.

Now I glare at her and say, "We need the stairs, Mum. It's basic."

"Stop fussing and decide which of these should go to charity and which we should keep."

I look down at the heap. "You decide," I say in a weary voice, and go on down the landing to my bedroom.

I push the door. Usually it swings open, but today it won't go more than a few centimeters.

"What the... Mum! I can't open my bedroom door!"

Mum doesn't answer, and I get a horrible sinking feeling as I push into my room.

"No way!"

I can't believe it. Piles and piles of sacks have appeared in my room while I've been out at school and then on my paper route. My desk is completely covered.

"My English coursework!" I scream out, trying to push things off the desk, but there's just no room anywhere. Even the window's covered with a stack of boxes reaching almost to the ceiling.

A huge pool of anger whirls up through me as I go back down to Mum's room and roar, "What have you done? Don't you care about anyone but yourself?"

"The planet," she starts, and I let out a high-pitched scream.

That stops her and she stares at me, her eyes wide open.

"I'm sick of the planet! I hope it blows to a million pieces and your collection with—"

"Josie! What a terrible thing to say. I can't believe—"

"Well, you'd BETTER believe it!"

Mum just sits there, her mouth shaped into a big *O*, as if she's surprised.

I can't stand it. I turn back downstairs, and suddenly I'm picking up boxes, bags, piles of newspapers, anything I can grab. I'm chucking them against each other.

"Stop that right now!"

But I can't stop. Then a wall of sacks and boxes comes rolling toward me like a giant wave. Something sharp tears into my forehead. I put out a hand and grab what feels like a picture frame. It's got vicious corners, and that's blood on my face.

I turn the frame over and there's a picture of a pretty cottage in a garden full of flowers. Along the bottom in bright yellow letters is written THERE'S NO PLACE LIKE HOME.

"It's about time I moved out!" I yell, and with all the force I can muster, I throw the picture over the pile of boxes.

"You nasty girl!" Mum's face is looming over me.

"Me? Your collection's trying to kill me!"

"Oh, stop fussing and get yourself up. That cut needs a Band-Aid," she says, turning away and piling up the boxes again in an even more dangerous pile.

I'm out of here, I tell myself. I get up, squeeze down the hallway and out the front door.

The thought of swim boy with his golden skin and immaculate nails seeing me now makes me want to die of shame. I stagger down the street, almost blinded by tears and blood, and all I can think is, There is definitely no place like *my* home!

2.

There's a pharmacy in the parade of shops in the next street, and I go there if I need anything. Mum hates doctors, so we've never had one. Mel, the pharmacist, always gives me advice about period pain or anything.

Maybe she'll give me a Band-Aid now, I think, as I storm off down the road. I'm furious I might have to buy first aid supplies and cut into my savings.

I won't have dinner, I decide, and then when I pass out starving to death in front of Mum, she'll feel sorry she mucked up my room and clear the stuff.

But I know that will never happen. Mum just can't *see* beyond collecting. She goes to secondhand shops every single day, and now she evens works in one. She's like a kid in a sweet shop, bringing home more and more stuff.

"It's my principles, Josie," is one of her favorite sayings. "All this waste, everywhere you look. How long before the whole planet is one big rubbish dump?"

I've heard it all my life but somehow, since I turned fifteen last autumn, I find Mum's principles and her ever-growing collection harder and harder to put up with.

The kitchen was completely full to the door by the time I was ten. That's when I got my paper route. Food became unreliable. I've been showering outside the house since I started secondary school, and in the past few months I've decided to move out as soon as I can afford it.

The sooner the better, I tell myself now as I reach our local shops.

"What happened to you?" calls out Mel as I go in the pharmacy and the little bell chimes.

The shop's empty, which is a relief.

"Tripped," I say. The tissue I'm holding to the wound is disintegrating.

"Let's have a look." Mel comes around the counter, pulling on plastic gloves like a paramedic. She has very straight blond hair that gleams in the fluorescent lighting, and she's wearing a clean white coat. I feel as though I'm messing up the place.

She splits open an antiseptic wipe and dabs at the cut. "It's not deep. Just needs a Band-Aid. Hold that."

I put my hand over the wipe as she goes off and gets a Band-Aid. Once she's smoothed a see-through one over the cut, I feel much better. I peer into one of the shaving mirrors on the shelves. Doesn't look too bad. Will swim boy notice? I want to go back to the pool tomorrow and see if he shows up. Why would anyone go swimming every single morning? I shiver at the thought.

"Saw your mum in a secondhand shop this week. She was buying a lot of stuff," comments Mel. She's back around her side of the counter, tidying up the cough medicines.

"Tell me about it," I groan.

It's after seven and I'm starving. On Friday night we usually sit on Mum's bed, have fish and chips, and talk about our week. Mum's a vegetarian, of course, because she doesn't believe in keeping animals for food and ruining the land. But she makes an exception for fish. I eat anything.

Should I go home? I wonder, feeling utterly miserable.

"Where does she put it all?" says Mel, and something about her tone makes my skin crawl.

"Our home is no one's business," Mum's told me all my life. "Once we close the door we are in our own special world. Don't tell your friends; they wouldn't understand."

Which translates into don't bring them around. So I never get invited. I've never been to a sleepover in my whole life.

Or had a boyfriend, Josie Tate, whispers a little voice in my ear. I picture swim boy looming over me, with his long golden body and those lonely almond eyes.

"Where could I get a swimsuit this late?" I ask Mel.

She looks me up and down for a moment and then she says, "I've got one you can have."

"Borrow?"

"No, actually, it's brand new; a friend gave it to me. I'm not a swimmer. You can have it if you want."

What if I hate it? I think, but beggars can't be choosers. "Great. Thanks."

"I'm just closing, so you can come up and get it."

In a few minutes we're out of the shop and Mel's putting a key into a front door.

As she opens it someone calls out, "All right, Mel. How's your grandparents?"

It's a man lounging in the doorway of the pet shop two doors down. He's almost bald, has a huge belly and his trousers are held up by suspenders.

"They're fine, Ron," snaps Mel. She pushes the front door, jerks her head at me and almost slams it shut. "Always poking his nose in," she mutters as I follow her upstairs.

We go into a living room with two very old-looking people,

a woman who's flicking through a magazine and a man staring at the TV. The man doesn't move or turn to look at us.

"Ooh, visitors, how lovely. I'm Ivy and this is Len. Who are you, dear?" says the woman.

"Josie," I say. "I live down the road."

Mel has disappeared, and Ivy chatters on and on. Everything about her is miniature; her legs are short and thin in her old-lady tights, her shoes would fit a six-year-old, and her face, which is very lined, is not much bigger than a large doll's face. Even her voice is a bit high-pitched, as though her throat only lets out tiny sounds.

Just when I think I can't listen anymore, Mel returns, holding out a green swimsuit with a black stripe going diagonally across the front.

"Ooh, matches those lovely green eyes of yours," says Ivy.

"What do you think?" says Mel.

"Are you sure? I could give you, er, something for it." It must have cost a fortune. There's a tiny expensive-looking logo on the side.

"Nope, it's all yours," says Mel, and then something about the way she looks at me makes me feel it's time to go.

"Thanks, Mel." Nodding at the old couple, I say, "Nice to meet you both."

The old man doesn't move. Ivy beams and tells me to come up anytime, but Mel's already moving toward the door.

As I walk home I think about Mel's flat, just like the one I want someday. She might have her grandparents staying at the moment, but otherwise she's got it all to herself. She's not married—she's maybe only twenty-three or twenty-four—that's just about ten years older than me. But she's in control of her whole life. Her flat gleams like her white coat. There's hardly anything in the living room—two armchairs, a small sofa, a TV, a dining table with four chairs. No shelves, no boxes, no plastic bags.

That's what I want. I just have to finish school and get a job so I can live like Mel. I don't even have grandparents to clutter the place up.

Mum's at the bottom of the stairs when I open the door, where she's banging a nail in the wall. Her green eyes look awash with tears, and I feel a pang of guilt.

"Fish and chips?" She finishes banging and offers me a ten-pound note.

After Mel's immaculate appearance, I can't help thinking how shabby she looks. Mum's hair is light brown, like mine, only longer and even more frizzy. She puts it up in a neat bun to go out and always dresses smartly, even to work in the secondhand shop. She likes two-inch heels at least. But in the house, she lets her hair hang loose and shaggy around her face.

"All right," I say.

She gives me a little smile, suddenly looking so fragile standing next to a great pile of boxes leaning like that tower in Pisa toward her. But just before I turn back to the street I see her pick up a picture and hang it on the nail. I catch a flash of a cottage with flowers in the yard. The picture that sliced my head open.

"There's no place like home," she says.

I slam the front door behind me and hope it rattles the teeth in her head. Imagine if the immaculate Mel came in the house. Or swim boy.

When are we ever going to tidy up?

3. Tasha

"I want to vid you for my vlog."

"I didn't understand a word of that."

I give an exaggerated sigh.

Dom smiles and fiddles with the sugar packets.

With a brain like his he can't help being a geek, but sometimes I wish he'd just tune in.

"I can't be a filmmaker unless I practice, yeah?" I say.

"I suppose so."

"So I'm making a vlog. You know, it's like a blog only it's a *video* log. . . ."

"Oh right, got it." Dom's dark eyes widen, and he gives my arm a playful punch. "Good idea, Tish Tash."

That's the baby name he made up for me when we were little. We've been best friends since forever, so who else would I ask for my very first attempt at making a vid?

"I thought you wanted to be a singer, go on television."

"That's so last summer," I groan. "Come on, let's get started." I fiddle with my phone and set it on video mode.

"Can't." He's pushed his chair back and now he's standing over me, the only time he's taller than me. Dom's taking his time growing up. His voice hasn't even broken yet. "Homework."

"But . . ."

"No buts, not if you want me to come to the gig tonight."

Which is essential, because no one else will come. Only Dom stays loyal to our amazing local band, Rough Steel, and of course he knows I'm crazy in love with Rory, the lead singer. Dom comes to every gig and sort of jigs around with me when I want to dance, trying to get Rory's attention so that he'll dedicate a song to me. Which hasn't happened yet, but hey, maybe tonight?

"No sweat," I say now. "We can do this another time. I'm going to ask Rory for an interview. What do you think?"

Dom has black skin and large dark eyes, and it's not always easy to know what he's thinking. He turns slightly to untangle his leg from the chair. When he turns back, his face is sort of deadpan.

When I stand up, I'm looming over him, two inches taller, which makes me feel a bit goofy sometimes. But I've got narrow shoulders and thin arms. Dom's stockier, although he's quite proud of his biceps.

"Don't get your hopes up," he says.

"I'm wearing the killer outfit."

"That's all right, then," and he gives a snort as we walk out of Terry's Café and say good-bye on the pavement.

There's more than two hours before I have to start getting ready. As I let myself in through the front door of our flat, I can hear Mum and Chaz all loved up on the sofa.

"Tasha?"

I put my head around the living room door. "Yeah?"

Chaz gives me a grin, his arm around Mum, her head lolling on his shoulder. Mum's had loads of boyfriends. She keeps saying, "This is the one, Tash, I know it is."

She's already forty-three and Chaz is eight years younger,

but he's okay-looking and a good laugh. He took us to the fair last weekend and spent loads of money.

"You out tonight?" says Mum, pulling on her top so her bra strap doesn't show.

"Yeah," I say. Chaz catches my eye and gives me a wink. I give a bit of a laugh, and he frowns slightly and nods down to Mum. No idea what that means.

"I don't want you taking the bus home late," says Mum.

"She's a big girl now, Hev," says Chaz. He reaches into his shirt pocket, pulls out a twenty-pound note and hands it to me.

"Wow! You sure?" I say, a bit overwhelmed.

"Course."

"You spoil her," says Mum, flicking back her hair. She keeps it long, halfway down her back, and hennas it every month. She says it makes the men look twice, and I have to admit it does look good. "Are you going with Dom?" she asks now, craning her neck to look up at me.

"Yeah, his dad'll give me a lift."

"Dom's a good boy. He'll take care of you."

Yes, I think with a sigh, but I'd much rather the gorgeous Rory take care of me. A flash of his long, thin body, floppy red hair and cheeky, totally sexy grin wafts across my mind. I am *so* in love. He's only twenty and I'm very nearly sixteen.

"I said, pizza or curry?" Mum's asking me about dinner.

"I'll get myself a sandwich." As Mum starts to protest that I have to eat properly, I dodge out of the room and down the hallway to my bedroom.

Time for the first entry on my vlog, I decide, flopping on the bed. I open my laptop and click on the icon.

I stare at myself on the screen, and for a moment I don't

know what to do. I feel a bit like I'm on TV, which is totally stupid because no one else can see this.

I take a deep breath and start talking.

> Tasha Brown's Vlog
> Saturday, October 5, 4:45 p.m.
> *Little laugh.* Hi—no idea who I'm saying hi to. Myself, I suppose. This is my very first vlog, and the reason I'm doing this is to practice being a filmmaker because that's what I want to do when I leave school. I'll probably have to work my way up from tea girl or something, but one day I'll be on the set with a famous filmmaker like Sofia Coppola or Steven Spielberg, and the cameraman will keel over having a heart attack or something just at the most crucial moment, and then I'll leap into his place and finish the shot and everyone will clap like mad and say, "How amazing! She's so young! A precocious talent!" And I'll be made for life.
>
> *Pause.*

Phew! I'm all out of words! I press playback. I look okay, I think, although I need Dom's opinion. Not that he'd ever criticize me, he's so sweet.

I've just had my hair restyled, shaved at the back and hanging very straight halfway down the left side of my face. Sort of an arty, filmmaker style. The pin through my eyebrow looks good, and I've decided to ask for a nose stud and tongue bar for my sixteenth. I'm wearing my denim shorts tonight and the black tights with huge holes. One of the girls hanging all over Rory last Saturday had tights like that.

I finger Chaz's money. I could get some vodka and a couple of bottles of Coke and make some drinks, offer some to Rory. The thought makes me feel warm all over.

I press Play and continue.

> Well, this is my room.
>
> *Camera pans around room.*
>
> That's Mickey Mouse. I've had him since I was three. If you shout at him, he used to make a noise and move a bit, but it doesn't work anymore. That's my bed, and that's all my makeup, and the photo in the frame is my dad holding me when I was a baby. He got killed in an accident at work—I don't remember him. Mum says she can't be a widow all her life, so she dates all these different blokes. Now she's with Chaz and maybe they'll get married, so I can be a goth bridesmaid, all in black—bet Chaz would let me—and maybe they'll have a baby and I'll have a little brother.

I press Pause.

My mouth seems to be running on and on, but I can't help picturing myself at the playground, pushing my little brother on the swing and making him laugh. Rory comes past and sees us and thinks, Tasha would be such a great mother, and he proposes to me on the spot.

My phone goes. It's Dom. "Seven at the bus stop?"

"Yep. I've done three minutes, fifty-two seconds on my vlog."

"Cool. Laters."

Dom tries to be cool but just saying it isn't necessarily being it. He wants to be an engineer or a research chemist. He's doing A Levels a year early, and he's already thinking about uni. He's way ahead of everyone in our year and probably the sixth form too.

"Bit much, isn't it?" I said when he told me.

But his eyes glazed over and he said, "It's cool."

I take a shower and when I'm back in my room, I lie down on my bed in my underwear, hands under my head, and stare at the ceiling. I try to picture my first movie with the sound track by Rory and Rough Steel. Suddenly my bedroom door swings open.

It's Chaz, and he sees me in my bra and underpants!

I sit up and grab my duvet to cover up. He stands there staring at me. Then he shakes his head with a little smile and mutters, "Sorry, wrong room," and he's gone, the door still wide open.

I leap to my feet, shut the door and dress really quickly, without worrying about what Rory will think when he sees me. Why did Chaz do that? Crazy weird. Our flat's just a series of doors off a corridor. Anyone could make that mistake, I tell myself. When he smiled at me, it was a sort of fatherly smile, wasn't it?

By the time I've got my makeup on and slung my purse and bus pass into a bag, it all seems something of nothing, as Mum says when I moan. I pull on my black denim jacket, go down the corridor to the front door and call out, "See you later, Mum."

"Stay with Dom," she calls out, like always.

And then just like always, Chaz calls out, "Have a good time, love."

See? I tell myself as I go out of the downstairs door and onto the street. It was just a mistake.

I've got Chaz's money in my pocket, and I've already decided what I want. The little grocery on the corner isn't fussy, so soon I'm stuffing a small bottle of vodka and two bottles of cola into my bag.

"How old did you say you were, babes?" I imagine Rory saying when I offer him some.

"Eighteen," I'll answer, giving Dom a big kick.

But inside a little corner of me knows there's another reason why I bought the vodka tonight.

4.

"Put that away," Dom hisses as we get to the gig.

"It's just Coke," I say, and take another swig. I've drunk a third of the bottle already. My head's a bit woozy.

"What's up with you tonight? You're strange."

"No, I'm not. I'm the same." I offer him the bottle.

He shakes his head. "No, Tash, and you've had enough too."

I'm just about to call him a wimp when we're inside and Rory's right in front of me. This is my chance. I sidle up, hold out the bottle and say, "Drink?"

Rory's wearing a black T-shirt and faded blue jeans with a leather belt that almost matches his hair. He's way taller than me and he grins down, saying, "Is it diet?"

"No way! I mean, yes." I sound ridiculous. "Try it."

I offer the bottle and he takes it and drinks almost to the bottom in seconds. He comes up for breath, wiping his mouth with the back of his hand. "Nice one, babes," he says with a smile that zooms straight through me.

Babes. Yaay!

Dom's hovering around so I don't get out the second bottle. Rory's walked to the front and grabbed the microphone.

"So this one's for the little girl with the cola eyes." He's looking straight at me, and I feel like swooning, just like in the old black-and-white films. Would he catch me before I crashed to the floor?

They're playing "Angel Storm." I *so* love that part of the song when Rory hits the top note and the bass goes crazy behind him. I grab Dom and push him into a dance. I've got the second vodka mix in my hand, and I keep taking swigs. Dom's mouthing stuff at me and frowning but I ignore him.

I want to dance until the morning. I want Rory to kiss me. I want to finish all the vodka and send out for more.

Rory. Dom. Vodka. Storm.

The words are in my head, crazy weird, and they're pushing out the one word I don't want to think about tonight.

Chaz.

The song's over and Dom pulls me to a table. Everyone's high but Dom's hissing in my ear, "If Dad smells the drink when he picks us up..."

"Chill. He won't."

I sway a bit and put my head in my hands. Then I reach into my bag and pull out a stick of chewing gum. I put it in my mouth and look at Dom, my mouth wide open as I chew.

"Have you gone mad?"

"Nope," I say. "Just mad in love."

For some reason his head drops, probably because he's so annoyed with me. A couple of the girls from school call me over to join them, and I'm dancing again, passing around our bottles. We giggle and swig until it's all gone and Dom doesn't have anything to whine about anymore.

It's getting late, and the other girls leave.

Dom calls out, "Shall we wait for Dad outside?"

I ignore him. I'm still hoping something will happen with Rory.

"Tash?" Dom's almost whining, and I feel like batting him away like a fly. Why's he being like that? He knows how I feel about Rory.

There's a beer coaster on the floor. It's a bit damp but I pick it up and then I have a thought.

"Pen," I say to Dom, holding out my hand.

He looks up at me, the whites of his eyes suddenly caught in the strobe, making them gleam out of his dark face.

He's so much *younger* than me, I think, even though we're both sixteen in December.

Dom never leaves home without a pen. He's holding it out to me. I scribble my mobile number on the mat and walk over to Rory. There's a girl hanging over his shoulder, but the vodka's pumping me up. I hold out the mat to Rory and say, "Call me. Anytime."

Rory gives a little grin and he looks so gorgeous I feel weak at the knees. He stuffs the mat in his shirt, which is unbuttoned halfway down his chest, and says, "Cool, babes."

The other girl gives a titter as I turn away.

Am I ugly? I think.

The memory of Chaz's face looking at me in my underwear creeps back in and a chill goes through me. Then a hand slips through my arm. It's Dom, and the warmth of his body feels so good I flash him a grin.

"Okay, Tish Tash?" His voice is a bit deeper for once. He gets embarrassed when it suddenly hits a high note. He's still going through puberty is my little Dom.

I lean into him and he squeezes my arm. "Dad's texted me. He's outside."

Dom's dad is all smiles in the car, and Dom does the polite conversation thing about what a lovely evening we've had.

When we get to my flat, Dom says, "Go carefully, Tish Tash."

I give him a hug and get out of the car.

"I'm always here for you," he calls after me.

I don't look back as they drive away, but when I get to the front door I suddenly wish Dom *was* with me, which is stupid. He couldn't stay overnight; we don't have a spare room. We've been best mates since we were five and started in the same class at school. The teacher made us all hold hands with our partners to go into assembly. The girl next to Dom said, "If I hold hands with Dom, will my hand go all black?" Someone giggled and Dom's head dropped down. I marched up, took Dom's hand, and said, "I'm your partner now." I remember how he smiled at me all morning. My sweet little Dom always looks out for me, doesn't he?

No sign of Mum or Chaz as I tiptoe to my room. It's just gone midnight, and they must be in bed, sound asleep.

I undress quickly, prop a chair under my door handle—just to be fully private, I tell myself—and fall asleep under my duvet.

In my dreams a squirrel's scratching at my window for nuts. We haven't got any nuts, I think, and then I wake up. The sound has changed into a knocking sound. How can a squirrel knock on a door? I wonder, still half asleep. My head's thumping. A proper hangover. I can't help feeling proud of myself.

The knocking's more persistent. The time on my clock says two a.m.

"Open up, Tasha. I need to ask you something."

Chaz? God!

Suddenly I'm wide awake. What's going on? Why doesn't he ask Mum if he needs something?

I creep out of bed and check that the chair's stuck under the door, but he's rattling the handle now and I'm not sure if it will hold.

Then I hear Mum's voice calling out, "Is that you, love?"

The rattling stops and I imagine Chaz frozen in his tracks. I can hear breathing, but I think it's mine.

"Chazzie?"

"Coming," he calls back.

I hear him padding down the corridor and I collapse back into bed, my heart thumping more than my head. This is unreal. What did he want? I toss and turn for the rest of the night and by morning I decide to ask Mum about it when she's on her own.

I grab my chance around eleven when Chaz goes out to get a paper. Mum's buttering toast in the kitchen and flicking through a magazine.

"Don't you think Chaz is a bit young for you?" I say casually, filling the kettle.

Mum grins and shakes her head. "He likes older women."

Oh yeah? I think.

"He's a bit weird, you have to admit."

She frowns and drops the magazine. "Oh, here we go. I wondered how long it would take you."

"Mu-um."

"Don't Mum me. It's always the same when I've got someone..."

She's off like an express train, and yeah, I have been stupid in the past, getting jealous and wanting her attention. It's been a couple of years since she's gone out with anyone but this time it's different. Only I don't know how to make her see.

Direct action, I decide. "He came into my room yesterday when I was in my bra and underwear."

She cocks her head to one side, pursing her lips, which

means she's getting proper angry, and says, "I know. He said. He wasn't thinking and opened the wrong door."

"Yeah, well, why was he knocking on my door in the night?"

"I asked him to make sure you were home okay if I fell asleep. Honestly, Tasha. You're nearly sixteen. I'm really sick of this. Can't you be happy for me, just this once? I told you, he's the one. You'll be leaving home in a couple of years, off to college with all your mates, getting off your head and whatever students do. I'll be stuck here all on my own. Is that what you want? Is it?"

I shake my head, feeling really miserable. Maybe it *is* me and I've got it all wrong about Chaz.

Tasha's Vlog

Sunday, October 6, 11:21 a.m.

Nothing from Rory. I thought he'd send me a text. But he dedicated a song to me and called me babes, twice. I drank too much vodka, my head's splitting and look at those circles under my eyes.

Pause.

I reach across my bed for some eye gel and smear it on. It feels cool and refreshing. Can I say anything on my private vlog? Is it safe or will someone hack into my laptop and read it?

Chaz's name floats like a whisper in my ear. Mum thinks I'm jealous and maybe I am and that's why I'm down on Chaz. Or maybe he's—

My phone goes. It's Dom. "Yeah?"

"Just wanted to see how you're feeling this morning, Tish Tash."

"Okay."

"Lucky you. I thought you'd have a terrible hangover. What are you up to?"

"Just doing my vlog." And then I get an idea. "I was wondering, you know, if someone stole my laptop..."

"It's too antique to bother with."

"Hmm, maybe. Anyhow, listen, Dom, just as an example... if someone stole my laptop and hacked in, they could watch my vlog, couldn't they?"

Dom gives a bit of a laugh. "What's so private? Is it rude?"

"You're such a child!"

He goes silent. So I say, "Can't you see, it would be like someone reading my diary, so just put me out of my misery."

"Okay," he says in a more serious voice. "Anyone can be hacked. People have hacked into American Secret Service computers and ended up with thousands of years in prison. So none of us are safe."

Wonderful, I think. "So no privacy."

"Bottom line? Nope. Keep it in your head. Safest place unless they waterboard you. Gotta go, Mum's yelling."

I press Play and hiss toward the screen,

> If you've hacked in and you're watching my
> vlog, you're dead! Don't say I didn't warn you.

I grimace at the screen and wave my fist. I so wish I had a skull tattoo on my forehead or a razor blade through my tongue. But when I press Replay, I just look like a thin, grumpy, fifteen-year-old girl.

I'm in my own home and I don't feel very safe. Crazy weird.

5. Josie

Swim boy is standing on the poolside, dripping. "Glad you could make it," he says with a grin. "I'm Jordan."

He's wearing long black shorts that hang below his belly button and finish above the knee. Actually, I think he's wearing more than one pair, which is strange.

"Josie," I say, and grin back.

"Great suit, matches your eyes."

I blush. No one's ever mentioned my eyes before. I always thought Mum and me looked a bit like moth-eaten cats with our frizzy hair and green eyes. Not like Tasha Brown or Mel, with their hair so straight and well cut.

"Hope the water's warm," I say, rubbing my arms. Confession time, Josie, I think. "Um, I can't actually... you know... swim."

Our eyes meet but Jordan just grins and shrugs. "That's okay, I'll teach you."

My stomach does a somersault, but I'm not walking away now, am I? Not with Jordan grinning down at me. Anyway, it's time I learnt to swim, I tell myself.

"Here." He hands me a cap. "Everyone has to cover their hair."

How am I going to cram all my hair under this flimsy bit of rubber?

I can see Chantelle standing with a tall blond boy at the far side of the pool. She gathers her ponytail in one hand and in a slick movement flips the hat over her head.

"I'll put it on in a minute," I say.

"Sure. Try the water. Sit at the side and dip your feet in."

Jordan sits down next to me and we dabble our feet in the water. It doesn't feel too bad. The pool stretches away with white plastic ropes separating the lanes.

"It's a short-course pool," says Jordan. "Twenty-five meters, exactly half an Olympic length."

I nod and try to look knowledgeable. I know zero about swimming. "So, um, does everyone wear two pairs of shorts?"

He sticks his thumb in the waistband and counts, "One, two, three pairs today. They're called jammers."

"Right," I say. "That's a lot of layers."

"They're old pairs. The new ones have to be skintight to compete. After a while they go baggy, and then Coach makes us wear three pairs for extra drag in the water. They're like a wind sock, makes us work harder."

"Is he very fierce, your coach?"

"Insane," says Jordan with a short laugh. "Especially with my group, the Seniors. There's eight of us, and we all want to go for Olympic gold. So he makes us train real hard."

"How hard?"

"Like, ninety percent of the time, we're not good enough."

"Sounds tough," I say, staring into his almond eyes.

He stares back and says, "It's how we want it. Me, Chantelle, Taylor"—he nods toward the blond boy who's plowing up and down one of the lanes—"all of my group."

"So you all train every day?"

"Sure."

"You don't get bored?"

He laughs. "No time to get bored on my schedule. I came second in the European Juniors in July ahead of Taylor. Next year, when I turn eighteen, it'll be Senior International, then World Championships, and then..."

"Olympics?"

"Right." He turns back to me, his feet dipping up and down in the water, and says, "I want an Olympic gold medal, Josie. We all do."

He stares away down the pool and I can almost feel his hunger to win.

"Check out the clock," he says, and points toward a huge round dial with a hand steadily ticking around in seconds.

Suddenly he's in the water, streaking down the lane to the far end, arms pumping—and I don't see him take a breath once. The clock ticks around the black lines as he reaches the wall, doubles under and zips back to me. He comes up grinning, dripping water.

"Wow! That was amazing. You must be good enough for the Olympics."

"There's millions of trials before I get that far," he says, but his eyes are shining and I can see he's pleased I'm impressed.

"Twenty-four-point-six," calls out Chantelle. "Good time."

He nods over to her. "Everyone in the Torpedoes can do that," he says to me in a low voice.

"I can't," I say with a grin. Then, winding my hair up tight on my head, I wrench the horrible cap on. It grips me like a vise. "Okay, I'm ready."

Jordan glances over his shoulder. The rest of the team is leaving the pool area, and I see him relax.

"Walk down the steps over there into the shallow end and splash around until you feel a little warmer."

I adjust the straps of my swimsuit and go toward the steps. Jordan's in the water, and he pulls a couple of floats down off the poolside. I dip my shoulders under and come up shivering.

He hands me a pink float and says, "Walk to the other side holding out the float."

Once we reach the other side, he says, "Try jumping up and down. Feel the water holding you."

He jumps with me and it's amazing how far we spring out of the water, although he's miles above me. We laugh like a couple of kids, and I start to relax.

Water has its advantages, I think, even if this isn't exactly a hot bath. I'd love a hot tub when I get my flat, but you need a special room for that.

Then suddenly Jordan is behind me and his hand is on the back of my head. "Just lean back. Trust me, I won't let you go under."

"I can't."

"You can—just do it."

I'm terrified, but more than anything I don't want Jordan to take his hand away. His palm's cupped around the back of my head, and a thrill goes through me, like the little whoosh when I first saw him. I lean back slightly and then my body lifts upward as though gravity just disappeared.

It's amazing! I'm floating for the first time in my life. Maybe I will finally learn to swim. Mum never took me when I was little, and our old town pool was always closed for repairs. It wasn't until the council decided to invest in a brand-new pool and promote the county swimming teams that this pool was opened.

Jordan's walking backward along the width of the pool, and I'm staring at the ceiling, my hands whishing slowly back and forward.

"We'll have you in the Torpedoes in no time," he says.

"In your dreams," I say, and some water goes in my mouth. I splutter, my legs drift down and I'm back on the pool floor. "Sorry."

"It's okay, happens to me all the time," says Jordan with a laugh. "You have to learn to love pool water."

"It tastes disgusting."

"Have you ever swum in the sea?"

I've only been to the beach once. It took half a day on three trains from our town, and Mum didn't like the journey. She refused to go ever again.

"No," I say. "But then, I can't swim."

"Oh, sure, right. Stupid of me." His eyes have sunk in their sockets again, and his head drops.

Maybe he's had enough, I think. It was fun while it lasted. "Don't let me keep you from your friends." I nod toward the café, where I can see through the glass wall that Chantelle and the other swimmers are hanging out.

"Uh, no, it's okay. They're not my friends," he says, and then quickly adds, "I mean, we all get along okay, but I don't really have time, what with training and school and stuff. . . ."

His voice trails off and I wonder what he means. He must have some friends. "So, where do you go to school?"

"I don't," he says, ducking his head again. "I go to Portland College."

"Never heard of it."

"I'm not surprised. It's run in someone's house, like a

private tutorial place. There's only six of us doing A Levels. The others don't swim."

"So, they don't understand?"

"Something like that. They're all doing four or five A Levels, and they get together to study and talk about going to school—you know, uni. I'm doing history and English, and I want to qualify for the Olympics, so I don't have time for school."

"What do your parents think?"

He waves his hand around in the water and says, "They're sort of okay. Mom would prefer me to do science, go into research, you know?"

"Without doing chemistry?"

He gives a short laugh. "Mom's Japanese. All the kids in Japan study really hard and do PhDs and stuff. I've only ever been really good at swimming. Not like Crystal."

I raise a querying eyebrow.

"My little sister. She's top in everything, and she's a gifted piano player. Mom teaches piano, but she gave up on me a long time ago."

"What about your dad?"

"He's cool—believes in me."

"That's good," I say. "And you're American?"

"With Japanese eyes." He laughs. "Don't worry, everyone wonders. We come from New York, but Mom was born in Japan. We moved here when I was twelve because of Chambers."

"The IT place?"

"Yeah. Dad heads up the UK team."

They must be minted, I think, and then I rub my arms.

"You're cold," says Jordan. "Go and get changed and I'll meet you out front. No hurry, I'm doing twenty lengths first."

Twenty? I look down the pool. I can't imagine doing one length.

I decide to take a hot shower and wash my hair, drying it carefully under the hand dryer even though it makes it really frizz out. Someone at school said you need to cut long hair once a month to avoid getting split ends, but that's so expensive.

One day, I think with a sigh as I walk out of the pool.

Jordan's standing on the pavement talking to a tall man with broad shoulders and dark hair. They're about the same height.

"Josie, this is my dad."

"Hugo Prince," says the man. "Pleased to meet you."

He has that easy, expansive way Americans have of speaking, as though they're addressing an audience, but his hand and his voice are warm.

"Good to see Jordan's making new friends! So, come over for dinner."

My eyebrows shoot up and Jordan sees, his eyes sinking into their sockets again. "I don't think Josie..."

"Sure, she does." He checks his phone and then says, "Thursday's good this week. Jordan can pick you up."

"No," I say, and my voice nearly sounds like a shout. There's no way Jordan can come to my house.

Jordan's dad looks puzzled and Jordan looks so uncomfortable, I say quickly, "I mean, I'd love to come, but I'll find my own way."

"Independent lady, I like that," says Hugo, his face splitting into a grin, and then his phone goes. He puts it to his ear and says to Jordan, "Time to go, it's your mother."

As they walk off, Hugo calls out, "See you Thursday."

So, is that a date?

6. Tasha

Tasha's Vlog
Sunday, October 6, 2:33 p.m.
My hangover's finally worn off. I went back to bed and fell asleep. Woke up twenty minutes ago, haven't even brushed my hair yet. Mum said I was imagining all this stuff about Chaz. Maybe she's right. I need to focus on my film career. I'm going to ask Rory if he'll let me make a film about him and his band. That'll mean we'll have to spend hours and hours together.

Meanwhile I've been looking up all these sites on the net to post my vlog. Well, the bits that aren't private.

Pause.

I stare at myself on the screen. I look a fright. Good thing Rory can't see me now.

The flat's very quiet, and I peer out of my bedroom door. No one's around, so I drape a towel around me and skip out to the bathroom. Maybe Mum and Chaz have gone to the pub for lunch. He's off to Scotland in the morning, driving his lorry, and won't be back until Thursday.

I take a shower and I'm brushing my teeth when the front door opens and closes.

"Mum?" I call out.

No answer, but I hear footsteps in the corridor and they stop outside the bathroom door. I've left my clothes in the bedroom. My hair's still dripping but instead of drying it off I wrap a bath towel around me and grip it tight.

"Chaz? Is Mum with you?"

There's a silence, and I swear I can hear breathing outside the door. I think of that film, *The Shining,* where the woman's in the bathroom and the man's in the corridor brandishing a huge ax. My whole body's tense, my ears straining, and then the door handle slowly goes down.

I want to scream.

But I don't.

"Who's there?"

The door handle rattles a little and the door moves in a crack, pressing against the bolt. Will it hold? It must. What am I scared of? It's probably just Mum wanting the loo. But why doesn't she...

"Just me, love. You going to open the door?"

Oh God! It *is* Chaz. Where's Mum? I don't know what to do.

"I...I haven't finished yet."

"That's okay—just wanted to get something. Open the door."

His voice sounds so normal, as though it's the most natural thing in the world to come in while I'm in my bath towel. So why am I shaking?

Then I hear the front door again and Mum calls out, "Has that daughter of mine woken up yet?"

Chaz gives a laugh and says, "She's in the bathroom. I'm first in the queue."

Mum laughs back. I hear her outside the door and the sucking noise of their lips meeting each other. I whiz back the bolt, pull open the door and slide past them, snogging their faces off. Mum has her eyes closed but Chaz looks over her shoulder at me, and his eyes narrow a bit.

In that moment it feels as though my bones have frozen inside my body, and I can hardly get to my room. I slam the door shut and shove a chair up against the handle. Then I pull on my clothes, grab my bag, wrench open my bedroom door and, calling, "See you later," I go out the front door and into the street.

It's 3:20 on Sunday afternoon. There's no one to hang out with, so I decide to go to Terry's Café. Maybe I'm imagining all this. Dom says I blow everything out of proportion, but what if Chaz is, well, perving on me?

The thought's so horrible I stick my earphones in, turn the volume up full and walk down the street with Rory and Rough Steel booming in my head.

When I get to Terry's, there's just a couple of old men sitting at separate tables eating plates of mashed potato and stew. I order a tea and an egg sandwich. Mum's always going on at me to eat. I'm not anorexic or anything like half the girls in school. But Mum thinks I'm too thin. I'm a size six. I eat when I feel like it. Egg sandwiches are my favorites.

It's been ages since I did a sleepover, and I begin to think, Maybe I'll see if I can stay at a friend's house on Thursday night, and then maybe Dom's mum will let me stay Friday night because it's not a school night. I need to experience different lifestyles, I tell myself, for my film career. I start planning what to pack. It feels like I'm going on a special holiday.

I don't get home until after six, and Mum's all over me. Chaz is in the living room watching telly.

"Something to eat, Tasha? You know I like you to have a proper cooked meal at the weekends. I hope you haven't been stuffing yourself with chips."

I laugh. "As if. I had a sandwich in Terry's and hung out with the others." It's only a little lie. "When's Chaz off?"

Her back's turned to me as she dishes up a plate of beef and dumplings. I want to make her turn around, listen to me and look into my face. But she doesn't.

"Six tomorrow morning," she says.

I look at the kitchen clock. It's six thirty. Eleven and a half hours to go.

After I've eaten, with Mum chattering on about someone at work who's getting a divorce, she says, "We're watching a DVD later."

"I have homework," I say quickly, and she gives me a surprised look. "An essay I want to redo, er, do again," I say, feeling a bit flustered.

She doesn't seem bothered, and then as I get to the kitchen door I turn and say, "You know Chaz?"

"Yes," she says, picking up my plate.

"He isn't, I mean he doesn't..." I stop. I really don't know what to say.

"What?"

Perv on teenage girls, I think, but I can't say that, can I?

"Hate long journeys?"

She laughs. "Yes, course he does, but it's good money, isn't it?"

I duck out of the room and go down the corridor. The living room door's open and I hold my breath as I go past but Chaz doesn't call out.

Tasha's Vlog
Sunday, October 6, 9:45 p.m.
I feel as though I'm holding my breath all the time, listening, which is crazy. I haven't heard from Rory, but making the film will make him notice me, won't it?
Pause.

Is that someone outside the door? I thought I heard a scraping noise. Mum and Chaz sleep right at the end next to the bathroom, so they have to pass my door all the time. But there's only silence inside and the sound of the traffic outside my window, quite faint this time of the night.

Record.
I'm so tired. Sleep well and see you in the morning.

I must have fallen asleep straight away, but I wake up just after three a.m. to hear someone calling through the door. "Open up, it's just me."

It's Chaz's voice, really soft and, well, menacing.

I freeze.

Go away, I want to shout out, but I just lie there, the covers up to my chin, shaking.

He rattles the door handle, but I've got the chair shoved under it. After a while he goes away. At least I think he does. I don't fall asleep again, and then at six o'clock I hear the sound of the front door closing.

He's gone for now, but he's back on Thursday night.

Home just became an alien planet, and I don't have a laser gun or a Chaz-proof suit.

7. Josie

Jordan's house is a palace!

I had to walk miles along his road from the bus stop because each house is on its own grounds. They all have huge iron gates. I think I have to speak into an intercom to tell them I'm here. I press a green button, feeling like the girl from the wrong side of the tracks.

It took me ages to decide what to wear. I managed to sneak a shower and wash my hair in the phys ed block after school, but it's so frizzy it keeps escaping from the elastic and ending up all over my face. Finally, I decided on a green top and my black jeans, because they're almost new. I dropped by the pharmacy to ask Mel what she thought, but she was in a bad mood.

"I'm busy," she snapped when she saw me, so I scurried out of the shop.

A buzzer goes now and I stand there, not sure what to do.

It goes again a couple of times and then a voice says, "Push the gate now."

"Oh, yes, of course," I say and press the huge iron gate. It gives quite easily and I'm in.

The voice sounded foreign—must be Jordan's mum, and now she thinks I'm a right idiot, I think, as I walk over the drive to the house. The lawn's as smooth as linoleum and there are large pots filled with shrubs in front of the windows. The gate clunks shut behind me. No going back now, Josie Tate, I tell myself.

Then the front door opens wide and Jordan's dad is standing there, beaming, a glass in one hand and the other beckoning me in. "Hi there! Glad you could make it. Jordan's just changing. He swam tonight."

"Oh, sure," I say, and then wonder if he'll think I'm mocking his American accent. I blush and hover on the step.

"Come on in, through there," he's pointing to an open door and the sound of piano music is pouring into the hallway. "Crystal's just finishing up."

I tiptoe toward the door and peer in. There's a small girl, long dark hair flowing down her back, still in school uniform, playing away furiously at a grand piano. She finishes with a flourish and lifts her hands from the keys, holding them there for a second.

Should I clap? Before I can decide, a voice says, "You like Mozart?"

I look around and there's a lady with almond eyes just like Jordan's, same golden skin, jet black hair piled neatly on her head, black trousers with a knife-edge crease, tiny feet in gold slippers and a cream top. Her figure is just about perfect.

This must be Jordan's mum from Japan.

She walks toward me holding out a slender hand. "Nariko. This is my daughter, Crystal. My son you know, yes?"

She doesn't smile but her voice is quite soft, if firm.

I nod. "We met at the pool."

"But you don't swim. Do you play music?"

"I listen to it," I mumble.

So I've failed all the tests. How am I going to survive dinner?

"Come on, Mom, Josie doesn't need the third degree. I hate swimming." Crystal has closed the piano and come up to me. "I like your jeans, did you get them in *this* town?"

She only comes up to my shoulder, and she's quite petite like her mum. Her eyes are wider, but she has the same golden skin.

"I can't remember," I say casually, although of course I buy everything in the market.

"I only wear True Religion jeans. They're American. My cousin sends them over when she's grown out of them. She's a year older than me and—"

"Hi, Josie," Jordan cuts in as he comes into the room. "Sorry, you've met my annoying little sister."

He looks amazing in faded blue jeans with bare feet and a white polo shirt. His body look so fit and, well, toned up.

I give a nervous laugh and say, "Oh, we're fine."

I see Nariko tilt her head as if she approves. Phew, got that right, then.

"Beer?" says Hugo, appearing with a couple of bottles in each hand.

They're the small size. I take one and say thank you.

When Jordan takes one his mother frowns, but he frowns back and says, "One a week. Training," he explains, turning to me.

"Which is the excuse for everything," drawls Crystal. "Getting out of chores, homework, boring visitors..."

"Crystal," says Hugo in a warning voice.

"Oh, not you," says Crystal with a big grin on her face, and she slips her arm through mine. "Sit next to me, please, please."

I look around, confused, and then we're walking into the dining room, which is ablaze with a super-white tablecloth, crystal glasses and cutlery you can see your face in. Jordan sits opposite and his mum and dad are at either end.

It's like sitting in a restaurant at the Ritz. I've never been anywhere posh. This is just their everyday home life. How am I going to cope?

At least with Crystal chattering away, no one notices how nervous I am. Then Nariko puts a plate of tiny green-and-white rolls down in front of me. I have no idea which food group I'm staring at.

Jordan picks up a pair of chopsticks, grips a roll effortlessly and raises it to his mouth. He gives me a grin before he pops it in and starts munching.

"You eat sushi, Josie?" says Nariko in her firm voice.

"Um, sure," I say, although I have no idea what she's talking about.

"Copy me," says Crystal. "It's easy peasy." She picks up her chopsticks, prodding a pair next to my plate.

God! I can't do that!

I take my chopsticks in my right hand and try to grab a sushi thingy just like Crystal. I nearly get it to my lips and then the sticks slip and the roll flies onto Nariko's spotless floor.

Everyone laughs and Nariko and Crystal exchange a couple of words in what sounds like Japanese. Probably something like *clumsy idiot.* My face flushes red down to my neck and my eyes well up, but I can't run. I don't know how to get out of the gate.

Then Nariko leans toward me and says, "Please, pick up with fingers like Hugo."

I look down the other end of the table where Hugo is cramming the last roll in his mouth.

He licks his fingers and gives a loud laugh. "Trust me, Josie, I never got the hang of those damn things either."

I pick up a green roll and put it in my mouth. It tastes delicious, soft and slightly chewy. I finish the whole plate in seconds. "That was wonderful," I say.

Everyone laughs again but this time I laugh too.

Nariko disappears into the kitchen while Crystal clears the plates and chopsticks. When I look at Jordan he gives me a slow wink and that little whoosh goes through me again.

This is my chance, I tell myself, to have a real boyfriend for the first time in my life. I raise my eyebrows back. Jordan's eyes open wide and he's grinning at me.

The rest of dinner is like a feast. There's soup, chicken and vegetables, ice cream and chocolate cake. It's the best meal I've ever had.

"But the cake's the bestest," says Crystal in an injured voice, when I refuse seconds.

"So sorry, Mrs. Prince, but I'm absolutely full."

"No formalities here, young lady," calls out Jordan's dad. "Hugo and Nariko."

I blush.

Nariko says, "I will give you some for your mother. I make too much for the family."

Jordan says, "Why would—"

"Hey, son," cuts in Hugo.

There's an awkward silence. Then Nariko says, "Show Josie your trophies. Crystal, go with them."

"Yippee. I couldn't sit for another minute." Crystal leaps to her feet, and pulling on my hand, drags me from the room and up the stairs.

There's another two floors above us. It's like a hotel or something. The carpet's toothpaste white and I'm terrified I might have some mud on my shoes. I've noticed the whole family's wearing slippers.

"Should I take my shoes off?" I whisper to Crystal. Jordan's behind us and I hope he doesn't hear.

"Mom would appreciate that," she says in the most American accent I've heard from her yet. "Japanese never ever wear shoes in the house. It's not polite."

So why didn't anyone tell me?

I stop and slip my shoes off. Horrors. There's a huge hole in my left sock and my big toe is poking through.

"Don't worry. It's the same for everyone who comes here," says Crystal, with a completely serious look on her face.

Next time, I promise myself, I'm bringing slippers.

What next time, Josie Tate? I say in my head.

Jordan's bedroom is almost as big as our downstairs room and kitchen put together, only without the collection crammed to the ceiling, of course.

Crystal's chattering away as we go in. "Do you have your own room or do you share with your sisters or have you got brothers? I'd hate to share, but I love sleepovers. I bet you have loads of sleepovers with your friends. Maybe me and Jordan could come and—"

"Scram, Crystal," snaps Jordan, and her face falls. "Well, shut up then."

She grins and gives a little skip across the room. Phew, at least that saved me answering all those questions.

You have no idea about *my* house, I think, as Jordan waves his hand toward a shelf crammed with gold cups, plaques and medals.

"Do you ever lose?" I ask.

He gives a short laugh. "I try not to."

"Jordan's the top freestyle sprinter in the county and pretty soon he'll be National Youth sprint champ," says Crystal. "This one's when he was six and this one's when he was..."

"Crystal," Jordan growls.

He holds my gaze for a few seconds like when he winked at me over dinner, and I feel a warm glow go through me. We can be friends, I think. Like Tasha and her "sweet little Dom."

I've never had a proper friend. I sort of hover on the edge of things. Everyone's used to the fact I never get invited or invite anyone around. I know they think I'm a bit strange. Like saying what I did about Christmas in the bedroom last Friday. But it feels different here. No one's judging me, and I don't have to explain myself.

I drop onto the floor next to Crystal and cross my legs. We lean against the bed while Jordan puts on some music—not Mozart, an American band he likes. Then we all just talk about bands and swimming and how soon I might actually swim a whole length by myself. I don't notice the time until Hugo calls up that I have to go.

He insists on giving me a lift to my road but I manage to get out of the car halfway down. I stand and wave until he's gone, and then I walk to my front door and go inside. The house is quiet. It's nearly ten, and Mum's probably asleep.

As I squeeze down the corridor, past the cottage picture on the wall telling me there's no place like home, for the first time in my life I can hardly bear to be inside our house. The collection seems to close in on me, sucking the oxygen out of the air, whispering to me, *No room for you anymore.*

My bedroom's just as bad now that Mum's filled it up. I've

tried to move stuff out over the week but it's impossible. I gave up throwing stuff away years ago. Mum just takes it out of the bin and puts it back somewhere in the collection.

Imagine if Jordan or Crystal or his mum and dad came by. My home would make them all physically sick. Crystal would never want a sleepover here.

But it's Jordan who hovers in my mind as I roll under the duvet. Jordan with the almond eyes and long, strong hands, who held me safe as I floated in his blue pool.

It's nice having a friend. I'll never call him "sweet" or "little."

Friend? Whispers that little voice in my head. *Or boyfriend?*

A thrill goes through me, and then I drift off.

8.

I'm dog tired when I get home from my paper route on Friday night.

Mum's standing at the bottom of the stairs applying lipstick, and she says, "Come out with me, Josie. There's a new secondhand shop opening up and they're having a late night tonight."

"Only if we go and eat after," I growl.

I'm starving, and I can't help thinking of the wonderful dinner Jordan's mum cooked last night. It's years since we could get in our kitchen and make a piece of toast.

"Egg and chips in Terry's *and* dessert," Mum promises, putting her lipstick away.

Her hair's up in a bun and she's changed into neatly pressed jeans, red jacket, black knee-length boots and a handbag over her arm.

"Let's go," she says with a bright smile.

My mum's always well turned out, I think with a grudging pride as we walk to the High Street, her heels clicking on the pavement like a model on the catwalk. But then she's still young, only thirty two. She fell pregnant with me when she was sixteen, but my so-called dad disappeared. Her sister left home the year before and they lost touch, and their mum, my

Grandma Bet, died when Mum was eleven. Grandpa died when I was two.

That left my mum, eighteen years old, all alone with me and just Grandpa's house to keep us from sleeping on the streets. Mum's lost everyone in the world who ever mattered to her except me.

"That's why I became a collector," she told me once when I was nine. "Can't rely on people. All we have is the planet."

"You can rely on me, Mum," I said, feeling sad inside.

But she turned away to sort out a stack of newspapers.

She's chattering on and on now. "... They've just opened so they'll have some marvelous stuff. They always like to start off with a bang...."

"Don't forget we're looking for school shoes," I cut in.

"You can do that while I'm thumbing through," says Mum.

When we arrive at the shop, it's almost empty. I go over to look at the shoes.

Then I hear Mum squeal, "Josie! Come over here. You won't believe it. Look, it's just like the one I bought last year."

I turn around to see Mum holding a revolting glass vase with pink flowers all over it.

"Then you don't need another one, do you?" I say.

"Oh no, I must have it, I must. And this dear little chick." She calls over her shoulder to the bored-looking saleswoman, "I've got a hundred and thirty-three chicks at the last count. I collect them, you see."

The woman doesn't respond.

I turn back to the shoes, but they're the usual pile of scuffed castoffs with worn-out heels and soles. For a second a vision of Chantelle from the pool floats in front of my eyes, her long slim body in her swimsuit, hair sleek and ironed with straighteners. I bet she gets new shoes every week.

Mum pays the bill, and we go to the café. I help carry the bags of stuff. Mum has to buy everything she falls in love with: ornaments, another four skirts—"For work," she says—and six fluffy chicks.

"If we don't buy it, Josie, it will all end up in the landfill, and that's another bit of the planet ruined."

I can see her point but our house is *full.*

My stomach's rumbling so much I order a burger with cheese and bacon, a double portion of chips and a chocolate shake. Mum tuts about the burger, but I ignore her.

You have to pay at the counter and Mum spends ages fiddling in her purse. I go and grab a table and dump all the bags on the floor.

Then Mum comes over to me, flashing a bright smile, and says, "Give me ten pounds from your paper route money."

"What?"

"Spent it all, didn't I? You know how it is, Josie, don't you? And Friday's your payday."

I stare into her eyes, which seem lit with a kind of fever, a green flame like a meteor tail. She's spent all her money on her collection, and there's nothing left for *my* dinner. Again.

Saturday morning Jordan sends me a text. *Gone to Scotland, swim comp. Can't do lesson. Soz. JP*

I like that. JP.

But I feel miserable I won't see him. Maybe I should volunteer to help with the team, design their website (not that I know how) or give out leaflets or something. Then I could travel with them, and when JP is free we could . . . My imagination fails me.

I text back. *Hi JP. Hope you win. Will miss our lesson.*

Should I say I'll miss him too?

No. *See you next week. JT*

Well, that's cool, isn't it? I've never thought of myself as JT before.

I practice JP and JT in different colored pens. Green looks best.

My room's still stuffed with all the bags Mum dumped last week, so I decide to take my homework to Terry's.

The café's half full and there's the usual crowd from school around Tasha Brown with her sweet little Dom. Tasha's chattering away, and everyone's laughing.

Then someone says, "What about Josie? Her mum's got plenty of room. They've got a whole house to themselves."

"I thought you lived in a one-room flat," says Tasha, flicking her eyes my way.

"Why?" I say, my homework folders clutched to my chest like armor.

"Because you had Christmas in the bedroom."

There's a bit of a laugh and I shrug. She'd never get it, would she? How can you have Christmas anywhere in our house except in my bedroom?

"Tasha's into sleepovers," says Dom.

"Oh, not at mine," I say hurriedly. "You know my mum doesn't like people to come over. Anyway, why sleepovers?"

"If you want to be a filmmaker, you have to know how other people live. Durrh."

"You're such a drama queen, Tash," someone says with a laugh.

Tasha shrugs but she does sound a bit manic, I think. What's her problem?

"Anyway," says Tasha, "Dom doesn't mind. I'll stay until Monday, okay?"

She's looking down at her phone as she speaks.

That's a bit off. Dom looks stressed, as though it's not all as cut and dried as Tasha says, but he keeps quiet. What's going on there? But no one ever tells me anything. I'm not part of the gossip.

I think back to Thursday night, the three of us sitting on the floor in Jordan's room, chatting away about all kinds of things. I never do that, hang out with a crowd.

Sometimes it feels as if I live all of my life in my head. Like that's the only proper home I've ever really known.

The café empties out and I sit there, all alone, drifting through my homework, not really concentrating because I find myself wondering these days what mum's doing in the house while I'm gone. What if I arrive home one day and I actually can't get in the house?

I'm sixteen years old next week, and I feel as if there's no room at home for me anymore.

9. Tasha

Tasha's Vlog
Sunday, October 13, 11:46 a.m.
When it's just me and the camera, it feels like I'm talking to a friend. Only they can't judge or criticize or answer back.

I slept over at Tansy's house Thursday night and Shazia's Friday, but her mum said, "That's it for this term." Like, thanks very much!

Last night I was at Dom's. It's a bit crowded there. He shares a room with Jermaine, who's six. Todd and Davey, who are even smaller, are in bunks in a really tiny room and his mum and dad have their own room. But they gave me a sleeping bag for the sofa, and it was quite cozy. We all sat up and watched a late film. I didn't go to bed until after twelve.

I'm at Dom's again tonight, and then Chaz goes at six tomorrow morning and I'm safe until Thursday.

So everything's hunky-dory, as Mum says in her rock 'n' roll mood. The only cloud is Rough

Steel has a gig in Birmingham this week—
some scruffy pub, Dom thinks. So I won't see
Rory for ages. He hasn't rung or texted me.

Dom says he's probably lost the number. He looked quite pleased. Is he jealous? I've never thought about Dom like that before, but then he's never had a girlfriend, either.

Pause.

Mum and Chaz have gone out for the day so I have the flat to myself. I can catch up on homework, Facebook and everything and then grab my stuff and disappear before they get back. Mum hasn't said anything much about the sleepovers.

But Chaz did.

"Missed you last night," he said at breakfast this morning.

Mum was running water in the sink and didn't hear.

I pretended I didn't hear either, but I *hate* him saying things like that. I don't know what he expects, do I? I'm still not sure I haven't just imagined everything. I mean, Mum would know if he was a proper perv, wouldn't she? He can't be a pedo because I'm too old. They only go for children. Yuck.

I'm sixteen in December. You can get married with your parents' permission when you're sixteen.

Record.

Bottom line is, I can't sleep rough. They rape you. End of.

Being homeless without an actual roof over your head is what I'm MOST terrified of, so first thing tomorrow morning I have to line up the

week's sleepovers. Once that's done I can forget
about Chaz and his pervy eyes for another
week. Maybe he'll crash his lorry and end up in
hospital for months somewhere far away like
Belfast.

I sleep really well at Dom's Sunday night and wake up to find Jermaine and Todd climbing all over me, giggling and pulling my hair. Gross! I heave them off, nip into the bathroom, have a quick wash and pull on my uniform. You can't spend a lot of time in a bathroom shared by a big family. Not like in my flat. Well, not like it *was* in my flat before pervtime.

We all meet in the kitchen. Dom and I eat our toast leaning against the washing machine.

"Thanks for having me, Mrs. Jensen," I say to Dom's mum, sucking up.

She's got Davey on her lap, and she's wiping Todd's mouth as he kneels up on a chair, shoveling in cereal.

"Stop wriggling, Davey," she snaps. Then she says in a tired voice, "I'm not happy about Dom having friends to stay all the time. His schoolwork comes first, doesn't it?"

I feel a chill go through me and look at Dom. He just grins.

"I'm going to be a filmmaker," I say quickly, "so I have to have different experiences to broaden my horizons." I sound desperate.

She opens her mouth to say something, but Todd stuffs something disgusting-looking into it.

Dom says, "School?"

It's a relief to get out into the fresh air, even if it's raining quite hard.

"You home tonight?" he says.

"Yeah. Reviewing my vlog. I've done over ten hours of recording."

"Cool, respect."

"Honestly, Dom, what are you like?"

He grins at me as we push onto the bus. "I'll Skype you," he says as we go upstairs.

Not for the first time I wish that things were like they used to be. When we were in primary school, I went home every day for my tea with Dom because Mum worked until five in a supermarket. I'm too big now, I know, but if I was at Dom's most of the time, Chaz would forget about me, wouldn't he?

After school I go straight home. No Chaz, is all I can think. I'm going to take a long shower, do my nails, straighten my hair and pluck my eyebrows. It'll just be me and Mum for dinner so I might tell her something about my vlog and see if I can interview her.

I let myself into the flat, earphones in, Rory belting out "Angel Storm," and suddenly there's a big shape in the kitchen doorway blocking my path.

Chaz!

"Wha...what are you doing here?" I stammer, pulling out my earphones.

I'm staring up at him, and I swear he's leering down the front of my school blouse. I pull my coat around me.

Mum calls out from the kitchen in a cheery voice, "Chaz has a few days off. I'm going to throw a sickie tomorrow so we can do something together."

Chaz says nothing.

I push past him and into my room, jamming the chair against the handle.

That frozen feeling has returned. I throw myself onto my

bed, still in my jacket, and curl up into a ball, hugging Mickey to my chest.

I must have fallen asleep, because when I wake it's quite dark and there seems to be some sort of storm raging. Lightning streaks outside the window. I didn't even bother to close the curtains, and I can hear the rain lashing against the glass. Usually I love being at home in a storm, all cozy with the curtains closed. Mum and I used to turn the telly up loud and have a little party with Coke and chips.

But nothing feels cozy in my home anymore.

The time on my clock says 8:15. I'm still clutching Mickey Mouse to my chest. I start thinking about who I can call and casually suggest a sleepover tomorrow night. They'll think I'm weird. Totally crazy weird. But if Chaz isn't driving off for days, Oh God, maybe not until *next* Monday, that's a load of sleepovers to organize.

I tuck Mickey under my arm, grab a pen and a bit of paper and start a list. My hand's shaking.

Sleepovers

Tues. Tansy? Almost possible. Wants to be a film star. Offer her a part in my next short film.

Wed. Shazia. I know her mum said no more this term, but I could beg?

Thurs. Dom

Fri. Dom

I feel my eyes well up. Dom's mum doesn't want me either. My options are closing. Maybe I should run away to Birmingham and find Rory and offer myself as a roadie.

There's the most horrendous crack of lightning, as though it's just about to crash through my window, and I give out a bit of a scream.

My door handle rattles. "Tasha, love. You okay?"

It's Chaz, and before I can get to the door and check it's properly jammed, he's pushed it open and the chair has slid to the floor.

He's standing there in jeans and a shirt and he's staring at me in that pervy way of his.

"Get out," I say, but my voice is all weak and croaky, and I feel like crying. "I'll scream. And Mum will hear."

"She's popped out for a drink with the girls. Come on, Tasha, be nice."

He reaches out and strokes my cheek as if he's my boyfriend or something. Gross.

I'm still wearing my ankle boots, the ones with metal tips. The teachers are always calling me a rebel when I wear the wrong school shoes. Now I'm really glad I'm not regulation. I swing my leg back and throw it forward, kicking Chaz's shin with all my strength.

He lets out a loud yelp and buckles down, grabbing his leg.

I pick up my schoolbag and, with Mickey still under my arm, I make for the door. I'm down the corridor and out of the flat, leaping the stairs three at a time, and onto the street in seconds.

The rain's like a typhoon, lashing me and dragging my hair every which way. I'm drenched in minutes, but I don't care. I run and run and run. Lightning seems to be following me as I race through the streets until I come to a road that is vaguely familiar.

The house at the end. Number six. Of course, it's Josie Tate's house. I teased her into giving me her address on Saturday when she said she didn't live in a one-room flat. She and her mum have a whole house. They can't refuse to take me in. Not on a night like this.

I grab the knocker and start banging and banging. "Come on, Josie!" I'm screaming. "Let me in before I drown."

Or before Chaz comes.

10. Josie

When I get home from my paper route on Monday, it's after six and my feet are soaked. I've stuck chewing gum in the hole in my shoe, but it's not much use.

"Mum?" I call out in a grumpy voice as I push the front door shut and start toward the stairs.

No answer.

That stokes me up and I yell even louder, "MUM!" I push my way upstairs, not caring if some of the bags and boxes tumble down behind me. "When are we going to get new school shoes? My feet are drenched."

Still no answer, and when I get to Mum's bedroom door it's shut tight. I hesitate, listening. No sound, no radio or Mum whistling to herself, which usually drives me mad. For the first time in my life I actually knock on her door. Nothing.

The silence in the house is even deeper.

Pushing the handle down, I edge the door open and put my head around. The room's empty—well, as empty as any room can possibly be in our house. What I mean, of course, is that Mum's not there. She definitely isn't in the bathroom either.

It's too late for her to be in the secondhand shops; they all shut by five thirty. Mum might not have a job right now, but she always finds enough cash to spend on her collection, every single day, even Sundays. "You can't be halfhearted about saving the planet, Josie," she loves telling me. "You can never let up, not for a single minute."

"Except there's no room left in our house," I've been saying for the past year.

Last week when I almost *spat* the words at her after she filled up my room, she gave me a really strange stare and said, "Why should you care? You're sixteen in two weeks."

"What does it matter if I'm sixteen or six?" I yelled back.

I edge backward out of Mum's room now and head down to mine. The door opens more easily because I've managed to clear some of the stuff she dumped last week. But Mum's not there either, and suddenly my entire house, filled to the brim with Mum's collection, feels more empty than I've ever known it before.

The theme tune to *Star Wars* starts up. It's my phone. I pull it out of my pocket, and an unknown landline number comes up. I stare at the screen for a minute, thinking, Who's that?

Then I press the button and say, "Yes?"

"Listen, Josie." It's Mum, and she's speaking really fast in a funny, breathy sort of voice. "I've been sent to prison, as we thought might happen, for six weeks, because I didn't pay my council tax. But I know you're safe with Aunty Mary in Hull. I'll ring again when they let me."

Before I can open my mouth to speak, she hangs up.

There's a huge roll of thunder that rattles my window. Lightning streaks across the sky so close I think it's going to come in and strike me down dead.

Prison! What?

And who's Aunty Mary? I don't even know where Hull is.

Rain's beating like a hammer against my window, and the

thunder and lightning's getting closer. It's like I'm being punished for something, but I don't know what.

I'm home alone in a house filled to the brim with stuff my Mum's collected since I was little, and *she's* in prison.

Now what do I do?

Tears begin to well up in my eyes. I slump down on my bed. Is this what Mum meant? I'm old enough to look after myself now. Maybe she wants me to leave home. She was pregnant with me at my age, and *she* was all alone. Now we have nobody to turn to.

Correction. *I* have nobody. Mum has a prison full of people, three meals a day and no bills to pay.

What happens to fifteen-year-olds who are left home alone?

An awful picture comes into my head. Orphanages! Social workers come and drag kids away, screaming. . . . Well, no, that's only little kids, isn't it? But maybe I'll end up in foster care.

All these thoughts are competing with thunder and lightning crashing around the house like a dragon desperate to come in and consume me with fire and blood.

I'm starving hungry. I thought Mum might phone for a Chinese takeaway tonight, and I'd been planning my menu all the way home to help forget my wet feet. I wanted vegetable spring rolls, sweet-and-sour chicken, egg fried rice and beef with oyster sauce. Mum would have added vegetarian Singapore rice noodles.

My stomach rumbles at the thought. Maybe I can find some money in her room, I think, but I don't get off the bed. I've never in my whole life poked around in Mum's room. She's a very private person. She won't even open the front door if someone's in the street.

But then I look at her collection, which has invaded my

private space, and say out loud, "She broke the rules, Josie Tate. It's gloves off now."

I wipe my eyes and go to Mum's room. Strangely, her handbag is still on the bed near her pillow. Inside I find her mobile and wallet. Her whole life's here, and she never goes out without it.

Then I realize. Mum had to go to court today, and she thought she wouldn't be coming home. So she left her bag for me to find.

I pull out the wallet and open it. My eyes go wide. There's a wad of notes and the purse section is bulging. I count £110.00 in notes. When I spill the change onto the bed, there's mainly one- and two-pound coins.

Dinner is all I can think as my empty stomach growls again.

I phone the Chinese restaurant. They say they'll deliver once the storm's moved on.

I go back to my room, lie down on my bed and stare at the ceiling. It's pitch-dark outside, and my clock shows 8:30. My mind's a whirl as I wait for a thump on the door from the delivery man. I'm scared, hungry, confused and horribly lonely. Mum didn't even tell me which prison she's in. How do I find her? Do they have visiting times like in a hospital?

I must have dropped off because I wake up with dribble down my cheek and the sound of mad thumping on the front door. I get up and go downstairs. The storm sounds even worse—the windows are rattling and there's a pool of water on the tiles behind the door. Water always leaks in when there's a bad storm.

I can hear a voice outside—it sounds like a girl's. Strange. Delivery's usually by men in huge bike helmets. Why send a girl out in this storm?

I pull open the door and peer out, blinded by the wind and rain that soaks my hair and whips into my eyes.

"Josie, let me in. Now!" screams a high-pitched voice.

I push my hair away. Tasha Brown's standing there drenched to the skin, with a schoolbag slung over her shoulder and what looks like Mickey Mouse under her arm.

"Why . . . what . . . why are you here?" I blurt out.

She's pushing forward. I try to close the front door, but she's got her foot in it. Panic sweeps through me. We *never* let anyone through our front door.

"Come *on,* Josie, can't you see I'm drowning out here!"

"You can't come in, my mum doesn't like visitors. . . ."

"Shut up and let me in! I have to come in, Josie. I can't stay out here."

Her eyes are wild. She's throwing nervous looks up and down the street.

"Is someone after you?"

"What? How did you . . . ?" Then she stops, and a crafty look comes over her face. "Yes! There's a man, he's been following me, trying to grab me. Quick, in case he comes after you too!"

I must admit it sounds very scary. So I stand back, and Tasha squeezes through the door. I close it behind her.

We're standing almost nose to nose in the crammed corridor. Then Tasha takes a couple of steps farther into the house.

She gives a low whistle and grins over her shoulder at me. "You got a lot of stuff."

"My mum recycles," I say quickly.

"Okay," says Tasha, with a snort.

She wriggles farther into the house. The living room door is closed, but she gives it a push. Of course it won't open; it's full.

"We don't use that room," I mutter.

Tasha says nothing but she gives me a long stare. Then she moves farther in and stops before the stairs, peering forward. "What about the kitchen?"

"Er, no. Look," I say, getting really annoyed now, "you should ring your mum to come and get you. Like I said, my mum doesn't like visitors."

I sound like a right cow. No wonder I don't have any friends.

But Tasha stiffens and says, "She's away. She's got a new boyfriend, and they've gone to Spain."

"Oh," I say, thinking desperately.

Tasha starts to poke around in a box.

"Don't do that!" I snap but she ignores me. I've got to get her out of here. "Look," I say, "I thought you were having loads of sleepovers with your mates, you know, for your film career, so give Dom a ring."

But Tasha isn't really listening. She's peering all around the stairs and the kitchen and back over her shoulder to the hallway. I can almost hear her brain whirring.

"Where did your mum get all this stuff?"

"What—"

"Did the neighbors give it to her?"

"We don't know the neigh—"

"How long have you lived here?"

"All my life, and it's not really any of your business."

"So does she go through the bins?"

I'm so appalled I just look at her and then I say slowly, "She rescues things from secondhand shops."

"Why?" She has this innocent look on her face, and for a moment I feel like slapping her.

But instead I mutter, "She believes in recycling to save the planet. She has very strong principles."

"Give me a break," says Tasha in this totally sarcastic voice.

"Sorry?"

"Your mum isn't collecting stuff, Josie. Haven't you seen those programs on telly? About people like your mum who never throw anything away until they have nowhere left in the house to sit except their beds?"

Suddenly she's pushing herself upstairs, and I'm after her, begging her to come down.

But she's at the top, and she calls out in a triumphant voice, "I was right! Bathroom, full; bedroom, only the bed free; second bedroom—"

"No!" I scream. "That's private!"

But she's already through the door. When I get inside she's sitting on my bed, back against the headboard, ankle boots dripping on my duvet, looking at all the boxes and black sacks piled up around the room. Thunder and lightning still boom and flash outside.

Then she gives me a smug look and says, "No wonder you never have anyone around. Your mum's an obsessive-compulsive hoarder, and you're too ashamed to admit it."

Just then my mobile goes. It's Jordan!

Now what?

11. Tasha

Tasha's Vlog
Monday, October 14, 11:01 p.m.
Can you believe it, no wifi here! I didn't think *anyone* lived without wifi. But there's a bunch of students in the house next door, so I've managed to log into theirs. No password, the idiots.

This is the most crazy weird place I've ever seen, and there's no sign of Josie's mum. Josie said she's gone to visit some aunt in Hull.

But I don't care. I've got a roof over my head. Josie's given me her room and she's sleeping in her mum's bed, which is half covered with plastic sacks overflowing with fluffy toy chicks. Insane. Josie says her mum's saving the planet, so I had to put her straight. No she's not, I said. Your mum's a hoarder and she needs that psychiatrist bloke on telly to sort her head out.

Josie also needs a big Dumpster to chuck everything out, but I didn't tell her that because she screamed at me, "If you want to stay here you respect my mum!" Sounded almost like those gangsta boys who go on about respect. Or my sweet little Dom.

Pause.

My bottom lip's starting to wobble and I don't want to cry on my vlog, but just saying Dom's name out loud makes me feel so lonely. I wish Dom was here even though there's nothing he can do about Chaz. Dom's even shorter than me. But his lovely fresh smell of clean laundry and cinnamon—his mum makes pancakes sprinkled with cinnamon and sugar most mornings—would wash away the stale smell in Josie's house. You can't even see the windows in this dump, let alone open them. My mum's crazy about airing the flat every day, even when it snows.

Why hasn't Mum rung? I've checked my phone a million times, but no text, missed calls, nothing. Chaz has got her wrapped around his little finger and I'm practically homeless. I had to work really hard on Josie to let me stay here this week.

She doesn't seem to know how long her mum will be away. It's a bit weird her being left home alone, but what do I know? We're not friends or anything. Josie Tate's just someone who's always been around, but she doesn't hang with anyone. Now I can see why. You couldn't exactly have a sleepover in this dump.

Record.

This is my plan for the week until Chaz gets back in his lorry again. I'll persuade Josie to let me stay here until Friday. That will give me enough time to suck up to Dom's mum for the weekend. Chaz'll be gone starting next

Monday, so I can go home and start working on
Mum to try and get her to see what's going on.

I've still got my school clothes on and
maybe Josie will lend me something for the
evenings. There's enough stuff here; I probably
just have to rip open a couple of sacks,
although is it clean? Yuck. On telly when they
show a hoarder's house, they always find fleas
and rat droppings. Disgusting. But anything's
better than sleeping on the streets and getting
raped. I have to stay here however bad it gets.

I fall asleep in my underwear clutching Mickey. Then Josie's tapping on the door.

"Tasha, it's nearly seven. I have to do my paper route before school. You'd better go back home tonight before it gets dark so that man can't find you. Slam the front door hard when you go out."

Then I hear a loud bang downstairs, and she's gone. I'm all alone in the hoarder house. My mouth feels dry. The room's totally dark because the windows are covered with boxes. I get up, put on the light and look around.

In between all the boxes and sacks, Josie has a big bookcase crammed with books, a desk with what looks like English coursework in a thick file and a battered chest of drawers. I hung my tights up last night. They've dried out. I pull my clothes on and go down to the bathroom for a quick wash. The bathroom's insane. There's a cold tap free, but the rest of the sink is blocked up and you have to climb over boxes to sit on the toilet. Forget the bath. It's stuffed.

I swill some water around my face and mouth and go back

to the bedroom. Still half an hour before I need to leave for school.

Then it dawns on me. This is my big chance. I could make a film about living with a hoarder and sell it to a TV network for shedloads of cash. I can just see the headlines: "Fifteen-Year-Old Schoolgirl Makes Smash-Hit Documentary."

I grab my laptop, tuck Mickey under my arm—somehow he makes me feel safer—and press Record.

> Here's my temporary home for the week.
> *Camera pans around Josie's bedroom.*
> I am in the house of a hoarder, and as you can see, everywhere is stacked to the brim. This is the bedroom of fifteen-year-old Josie Tate.
> *Camera pans out into the hallway.*
> This is the upstairs landing, hardly any room to squeeze anywhere.
> *Camera pans around into bathroom.*
> And this, believe it or not, is the bathroom—but don't come around here needing a bath. I have no idea what hoarders do for a good wash.
> *Pause.*

I feel a bit mean when I say that. I don't think I've ever noticed Josie smelling bad, even though I don't exactly get close to her. But where does she shower? And what about cooking dinner? Last night after I'd arrived and she'd agreed I could stay, a massive Chinese takeaway was delivered and we shared it. Josie didn't even ask for any money, which was a good thing because I haven't got a cent. My purse has my bus pass and nothing else. Mum was supposed to give me money for the week, but she forgot yesterday morning. Then I didn't see her again before I had to flee the resident monster.

All this makes me think of breakfast, but all I can find are a couple of squidgy spring rolls left over from the takeaway. I eat those, go back to the bathroom and take a mouthful of water. Is that all the food I'll get today?

Then I have a brainwave. I ring Dom. "You awake?"

"Course. Mum's making cinnamon pancakes for breakfast. Jermaine's been nagging her since six."

"Ooh, wish I could have some."

Dom calls out something to his mum, and she calls back.

"Mum says come over."

"Be there in five!"

I'm out of the house and down the street at a steady jog, schoolbag on my shoulder, Mickey under my arm, glancing around nervously to make sure there's no sign of the monster. He wouldn't come this way, would he? Neither he nor Mum have even heard of Josie Tate.

How did Josie and her mum manage to keep this hoarder house secret for so long? There's a story here, and my film-maker nose is going to winkle it out somehow. I can't wait for Josie's mum to come back from Hull or Harrogate or wherever. I'm going to interview her if I have to tie her to her black sacks.

12. Josie

"We're on the run."

Ivy's looking at me with her tiny blackbird eyes.

"She's very tired," says Len, for the third time. He doesn't take his eyes off the screen.

Mel comes in with a tea tray just as Ivy leans toward me and says, "The Social want to put him in a home because—"

"Gran!" Mel nearly drops the tray.

"Don't be silly. We can trust Josie, can't we, dear?"

I nod. Wait until they hear my secret. "Totally. So is that why you're staying here?"

"It's no one's business," snaps Mel, and she does look really tired.

"I won't say anything, Mel. Promise." I stare up into her eyes, and she bangs the tray down.

"Len's, you know," Ivy goes on in her high-pitched, confiding voice, "losing the plot a bit. He couldn't remember how to tie his shoe this morning."

"Pants," says Len.

"Hmm," snorts Ivy. Then she goes on, "Liz, Mel's aunty, our *other* daughter, says he needs to go into a home. She sent the Social around, so we did a midnight flit, eh, Mel?"

"Midnight feast," mutters Len.

He turns around and stares at me. I feel confused and stare back.

"Now Josie will go and report it or her mum will," says Mel, "and Gramps will be in a home before the weekend. I *told* you not to say anything, Gran."

Tears well up in Mel's eyes. I feel so sorry for her that I blurt out, "Well, my mum's in prison and I'm home alone, and if you say anything I'll end up in a home too."

Mel's mouth drops open. Ivy grabs my arm. "Goodness, dear. Tell us everything."

"Josie!" Mel says in a shocked voice. She hunts around for a large box of tissues and wipes her eyes.

I tell them about the weird phone call from Mum, that I don't have an Aunty Mary and don't even know where Hull is. I haven't heard anything more since yesterday evening. I don't tell them about Tasha Brown and all the stuff she said about our house. She obviously knows nothing about recycling and saving the planet. My mum's just a bit unusual.

But I do know that I don't want Jordan coming over. He texted me last night.

Hi, JT. Swim lesson tomorrow night about six? JP

I stared at it for ages. I don't have time, I kept telling myself. But then a sort of anger went up through me. This is my very first chance to have, well, at least a proper friend for myself. Jordan says he's lonely too. In the end he'll probably realize he can easily get a really smart girlfriend like beauty model Chantelle, but right now I could use a friend.

So I texted back. *Great. JT*

I spent ages wondering whether to put an *x,* but I was just too scared.

* * *

I stayed awake all last night worrying about how to get Mum out of prison. At school today I went to the library. I spent an hour Googling prisons, but they don't give you lists of the inmates. I was too scared to ask the librarian in case she guessed I was home alone. But I'm missing Mum so much already. Last night I started to collect together things in a bag for her to take when I visit—if I ever find her.

Then I decided to talk to Mel before I go to meet Jordan. She's the only adult I know outside school. Maybe she can help me to work out how to find Mum and how to get her out.

"Bailiffs," says Len suddenly, and we all look at him. He's actually turned our way. He says in a more normal voice, "If you don't pay they send bailiffs."

"Len used to work for the council," says Ivy.

"I thought you said he—" I start.

"Gramps has good moments too," cuts in Mel. "Aunty Liz can't be bothered to help out, that's why she wants him to go into a home."

"So we ran," hisses Ivy.

"What does your mum think?" I ask Mel.

"She died last year . . ."

"So Mel is all we got," says Ivy, her tiny eyes gleaming.

Mel turns away for a minute and dabs her eyes again with a tissue. Ivy brushes crumbs off the table into her hand.

Then Mel turns back and says, "Well, have you had the bailiffs in?"

"I don't know," I say. "What do they want?"

"Take the TV," says Len. He crosses his legs and accepts a cup of tea from Mel.

You wouldn't know there was anything wrong with him, I can't help thinking.

"Anything valuable—computer, washing machine, car…" Len continues to list another load of stuff.

"We haven't got any of those things," I say in a small voice.

Mel gives me a curious look.

"They've given up," says Len. "So the court sent your mum to prison. Unless she's got a job and then they can take the money directly from her wages. Garnishee, they call it."

"She lost her job months ago," I say. "So how do I get her out?"

But Len's turned back to the telly, and Mel has to take the cup out of his hand, as it's beginning to tip.

"Please, Len, I need to know what to do."

"Not now," says Mel briskly, and she's ushering me toward the door.

I can't go, not yet. I need an answer. I hover in the doorway and stare down at Len, and then I lean over and touch his arm.

"No, Josie," says Mel in an irritated voice.

But Len, still staring at the screen, says, "Pay the debt."

Pay the debt whirls around and around in my head as I take the bus to the pool. How am I going to do that? It must be hundreds—otherwise Mum would have paid with the money she left for me in her handbag. Maybe it's thousands. It can't be millions, can it? I have no idea how much council tax is each month. I have no idea about bills—which is so stupid, Josie Tate, because when you get your own flat, *you* will have to pay them.

My head's still in a whirl as I change into my swimsuit and walk into the pool area.

"I won!"

It's Jordan. He's laughing up at me, arms spread out on the poolside, water dripping down his face, making him look even more gorgeous, if that's possible.

I stare at him for a second, my mind still on Mum and her debt, and his face falls.

Get into gear, Josie Tate, I growl inwardly. Putting a huge grin on my face, I say, “Awesome! Coffee’s on me.”

His face relaxes and I get into the water. We jog up and down the width of the shallow end as he tells me every single detail of his winning swim.

“…And just when I thought I’d blown it, I stretched my fingers out until I thought they’d drop off and I felt the side! First—probably only by half a millimeter, but…”

“It’s a win, who cares!” I say, puffing a bit. “Did you get a cup?”

“Medal,” he says, and his eyes are so deep and brown, the lashes lifted as they widen to full stretch, that I know he’s pleased I asked. “I’ll show you in the canteen. Chantelle’s looking after it for me. Didn’t want to risk the locker.”

“Oh,” I say, but I feel a bit of a pang.

“She’s going out with Taylor,” he says, looking sideways at me.

“Oh,” I say again, but I’m grinning up at him.

As I change and dry my hair I can’t help thinking, What would Jordan think if he knew my mum was in prison and I was home alone in a house filled up with Mum’s collection and invaded by mad goth Tasha Brown? Pictures of his immaculate family swim into my mind. I’ve got to get this mess sorted before Jordan finds out or I don’t stand a chance with him.

You haven’t even kissed, says a little voice in my head. Stuffing my wet suit into my bag, I shake myself and go off to the canteen. This is my very first chance, and Mum’s not going to spoil it, I tell myself firmly. I so wish I was eighteen, out of school and in my dream flat.

Trouble is, now I will have to use all my savings to get Mum out of prison and somehow find tons of money too.

13. Tasha

"It's *only* Thursday. I've hardly been here at all!"

"I didn't say you could stay after Monday!"

Josie's screaming at me from her mum's bedroom doorway. I can't get past her to the loo.

"It's only been a couple of nights. Christ."

"Three! You said you were going to Dom's from last night."

She's moved out into the hallway, and I'm trapped.

"Dom's flat's being redecorated," I say, thinking quickly. "They've all moved in with his aunty. There's no room for me."

"Then go home."

"Mum's still away, and she won't let me stay by myself in the flat."

Josie tosses her head and snaps, "What does she think we're doing here?"

"You said your mum would be back by Wednesday. How was I to know you're home alone? That's not allowed either."

Her head drops. That shut her up, I think.

"Get it sorted, Tasha. You can't stay here," she mutters, and goes back into her room.

I slither down the corridor, squeezing past all the stuff to the bathroom. I hate going to the loo with the door open but it's impossible to shut. I had to shower in the phys ed block the last two days, otherwise I'd stink. I think that's what Josie does sometimes, although I saw her stuffing a swimsuit into her bag the other day, so maybe she uses the pool showers. I'm not sinking to that. I hate swimming.

I opened a couple of bags in the bathroom when Josie was stuck in her room last night. I can't wear my uniform 24–7. I found a pair of jeans and a couple of tops that don't smell and actually fit me. But they're not exactly my usual style.

I sit on the loo with my feet on two plastic sacks and stare around me. How can they live in this mess? You can't even see the bath, and there's a massive biscuit tin crammed with soft toys balanced over the sink so you can only reach the cold tap.

I tried to move it on the first night and Josie saw me and yelled, "Don't touch anything! That's my mum's, and she *hates* anything out of place!"

"How the hell would she know?" I yelled back.

"If you don't like it, you can leave," she snapped.

Lightning was still flashing outside and all I could think was, I can't go home to Chaz, and I can't sleep on the streets. So I apologized about a million times. I haven't dared touch anything since.

But I have tried to open her eyes. Last night she ordered pizza and invited me into her mum's room to share. We were sitting on the bed, quite cozy really, munching away, and I said, "If you go on YouTube there's quite a lot of stories about hoarders."

"Shut *up,* Tasha. I told you, stop going on about my mum. What do you know!"

I was so amazed. Why can't she see? I know she doesn't have wifi, but she could Google it in the school library. It's like she doesn't want to find out the truth.

I looked up "hoarders" myself last night. There are some unbelievable stories. Apparently one in twenty people are hoarders, but all of them think they're the only ones. Hundreds of people just in our town must be living like this and you wouldn't know.

One teenager said she dreaded the doorbell going because they were terrified of people coming in and seeing how they live.

Josie doesn't even have a doorbell.

Another girl was never allowed to tidy up her own clothes, or her mum would go ballistic. She said, "My mum's a hoarder, my grandma's a hoarder and so was my great grandma." It's like an inherited illness or something.

The weird thing is that all these hoarders and their kids look just like normal people if you meet them in the street. I've seen Josie out with her mum at the weekends. They're always clean and neatly dressed. You'd never guess they live in this state. Crazy weird.

One woman had 730 tins in her kitchen. She'd just eaten a tin of meat ten years out of date. "It doesn't bother me; I eat anything," she kept saying.

I wanted to throw up.

The woman's mum had died when she was twelve, and she and her sister had nothing to eat. They found a tin of baked beans in the cupboard and each had one spoonful every day for a week.

"That's the root of your hoarding trouble," the TV psychologist said. "You started by hoarding tins of food and then hoarding everything until your house is full and there's nowhere for you to sit."

He managed to get the woman to agree to donate some of her tins to charity. She counted out thirty tins of beans and then she said, "These ten I'm keeping, but I'll give those twenty to the food bank."

I wanted to scream and chuck things at the screen. She'll never clear her hoard at that rate, I thought. It's so *frustrating.*

Now I wash my hands under the cold tap and go back to my room. Things are not good, if I'm honest. Mum has sent me a couple of texts, but when I try to talk to her on the phone about Chaz she just says I'm jealous and it's better if I stay with my friends for the week. I managed to sneak back home yesterday morning when they were both out and get some clean clothes. Mum had left me a note on the table with twenty pounds, so I'm not totally destitute.

But I'm just hoping that Josie's mum will stay away a bit longer until I work out what to do next.

My phone bleeps. It's a text from Dom.

Haven't seen you this week. Meet at Terry's? D

I feel my eyes prick with tears. I so want to see him, my sweet little Dom. I get all these funny feelings washing around inside me these days when I think about him. I can't imagine life without him, even though I'm proper in love with Rory.

Now I don't know what to say. I can't stay with him, not before the weekend anyway. His mum might not mind for Saturday night. Then Josie will think I'm making an effort.

Can't. See you Sat? x Tash

He texts back straight away. *OK x*

I thought he might send me a longer text; sort of beg me to see him. A large tear plops out of my eye and lands on my phone.

Mum doesn't care about me. Dom's wrapped up in his homework. Josie hates me and wants me out of her crazy weird house. Rory's ignored me. I don't feel as though anyone wants me anywhere.

Except Chaz.

I'm running back through my vlog when I hear a knocking downstairs. It goes quiet and then it starts again, only louder. Someone's banging on the front door. I wait for Josie to go down, but she doesn't. Probably got her earphones in. She likes to shut out the real world, I've decided.

Okay, I'll go down. Who cares if someone sees inside her stupid house?

I shimmy down the stairs, pushing stuff over as I go, but I don't care. I'm already sick of the hoard after three days.

I pull open the front door a few inches before it gets stuck on all the rubbish.

It's Dom!

I squeal and throw myself at him.

"Hi, Tish Tash. Couldn't wait any longer to see you. Soz."

His sweet, lovely, cuddly, dark cheeks and big brown eyes are laughing at me. I want to kiss him all over. Dominique Steven Jensen, my total best friend in all the world.

"How did you know I was here?"

"Emily said she'd seen you around Josie's house, gave me the address."

"Freckly Emily?"

"The very same and hot at maths," he says with a grin.

Maybe he fancies her, I think, and that gives me such a strange feeling—like disappointment or something. How crazy weird is that? They're the same height, I tell myself, and both geeks. It makes sense.

"What are you doing here? Sleepover?" says Dom, peering past me into the house. "Looks messier than my place."

I shrug. "It's okay. Josie gave me her room. Her mum's away for a bit."

"Come inside," I say. "And don't touch anything. They're very sensitive about their stuff."

Dom follows me into the house and pushes the street door shut behind him. I hear him suck in his breath as he sees the stuffed kitchen, and then we're clambering up the stairs. At one point a box falls behind me. I turn and see him catch it and carefully put it to one side. I give him a nod and he grins. My brain's whirling as I try to think of all the reasons to explain why I'm sleeping over here, but nothing sounds right.

At the top of the stairs I put a finger to my lips and he nods. We get past Josie's mum's door and are nearly at my door when I hear a shriek behind me.

"What's *he* doing here!"

It's Josie. When I turn, her face looks like it's going to explode with fury.

Oh God, I've had it now. She'll throw me out, and Dom can't take me in. My bones freeze just like when Chaz came after me.

"Hi, Josie, just came to see Tash for a few minutes. Hope that's okay," Dom says in his most friendly voice.

"No, it's not okay. My mum *hates* visitors and Tasha knows that and..."

Just then the *Star Wars* theme breaks out and she looks down at the phone in her hand. We all wait and then she puts it to her ear and says, "Hi.... Oh yes, great.... Yes.... No, can't talk now.... Okay.... See you Saturday."

"Have you got a date?"

I stare at Dom in horror and amazement. Why did he say that to someone who's so private she won't even open her front door unless you're about to be murdered?

Josie stares at him too and then she sort of rolls her shoulders as if she's all embarrassed and says, "Uh, well, yes, sort of."

"Cool," says Dom. For once he gets it totally right. Josie flashes him a grin, and those green eyes of hers, which are her best feature, to be honest, light up.

"Who's the lucky guy?" Dom presses on.

"Jordan Prince. Met him at the pool—he's giving me swimming lessons. But I can't go." Her head drops and she pushes a few buttons on her phone.

"Why not? Course you can. Where's he taking you?"

"That new gourmet burger place on the High Street."

"Random," says Dom in his best rappa accent. I wince but he carries on, "Burgers size of a brick. So what's the problem?"

Josie sweeps her hands down herself and says in such a despairing voice, "Look at me. Hair a mess, zero fashionable clothes, zero makeup—can't afford any of it. Jordan's rich."

I actually feel sorry for her. Not only does she live with a hoarder and can't accept it, but she has like absolutely no self-esteem.

I can sort this out, I'm sure I can. I'm racking my brains when Josie turns away, muttering, "I'd rather you go, please."

Then I get a brainwave. "No, wait! There's tons of clothes here."

She turns back and there's that green light again in her eyes. "What?"

"I bet I can find you a decent top."

"How do you know?" Her eyes have narrowed suspiciously. I can see she's about to get mad again.

"Look, I just had a peek when I was in the bathroom—couldn't resist—and trust me, there's loads of stuff."

"My cousin Angel's at school doing beauty and hair," chips in Dom. "She'll give you a makeup."

"Make*over,*" I say quickly. "We can make sure that Jordan falls totally head over heels in love with you, Josie—well, even more than he has already. What do you say?"

Please say yes, I'm pleading inside. I can tell from Dom's looks and tone that he's already guessing that this is no ordinary sleepover. I know how quickly my little Dom's brain works. By now he's put two and two together and come up with a mind-boggling formula that tells him I *needed* all those sleepovers. He's sucking up to Josie to smooth things over here for me until he's come up with a proper solution.

My eyes are wide as I stare at him. He gives me a slight nod, which Josie doesn't see.

"Are you sure?" says Josie in a small voice.

"Positive," says Dom. "I'm her favorite cousin. I'll make a quick call and let you know. Is it this way, Tash?"

He guides me down the hall and into Josie's room before Josie can protest any further.

I can't imagine mousy Josie Tate with her straggly hair and boring clothes scoring a decent boyfriend. He's probably some loser even if he's rich, but hey, who cares?

If she wants our help she has to play the game, and that starts with letting me stay here as long as I need to.

I have my sweet little Dom to thank for keeping a roof over my head. Trouble is, I can see from the look on his face that he wants answers. Lots of them.

14. Josie

I've just been asked out on my first proper date. I don't even want to go.

Jordan's voice was such a shock on the phone, standing in my house with Dom and Tasha. I feel so *invaded.*

After all these years of keeping our lives private, suddenly it feels as if the whole school is shoving through the front door. How much longer before Jordan comes here too? God! That can *never* happen.

And what about Mum? I don't even know what prison she's in. Somehow I have to pay her debt like Len said. After Mel almost pushed me out of the flat, she called after me, "You need to go to the council and ask how much your mum owes."

Then she slammed the door behind me.

When I got home, Mum's cottage picture seemed to be mocking me. *There's no place like home.* I ripped it off the wall and threw it so hard it sank out of sight behind the kitchen collection. Good riddance too.

It's hard to keep one thought going in my head for more than a few minutes.

Right now Tasha's decided she's going to find me an outfit to wear for this date on Saturday night. She won't take no for an answer. It's pretty obvious she's been going through some of mum's stuff. Every evening she wears a different outfit, and she didn't have a suitcase with her when she turned up in the storm.

"This," she says, flinging something behind her. "This, this and this."

Dom's on his mobile speaking to some cousin of his to do my hair.

They're a weird pair. Tasha only has to snap her fingers and he comes running. I heard her squealing like mad when he showed up at the front door. She sounded quite manic—desperate, I thought.

So what's that all about?

But I must admit it's nice to have some help if I'm going on the date. Just the thought sends butterflies around my stomach.

I look at the pile of clothes at my feet and pick up a pair of black shorts. "Too tiny, I'll never get into those."

Tasha tuts and grabs a red pair with glitter around the waist. "These'd fit you, easy. And this top."

It's a strappy black thing, not much more than a scrap of cloth. "I'm not sure..."

"This?"

"That's better." I take a slightly longer top with little sleeves and a huge purple heart on a white background. There's a silvery logo on the shoulder.

"I told you it was all designer," says Tasha.

I've never heard of them, but if Tasha's impressed it must be okay.

I try on the outfit with a pair of black tights, my last pair without holes.

"You look great," says Dom, putting his head around the door. "My cousin can do you after work on Saturday, about six thirty. Once she's finished, trust me, your man'll be knocked out."

Tasha flings an arm around Dom, and his brown eyes go liquid.

Then he's pulling himself away, saying, "Got to go, Tish Tash. I'll pick you both up Saturday. Mum says you can stay over."

The front door slams behind him.

Tasha gives me a shrug and says, "I'll be out of your hair."

A lost look hovers around her eyes, and it's almost as if she's pleading with me. There's another reason why she can't go home, I bet, but I'm not asking because there's no way I'm telling Tasha Goth Brown and her sweet little Dom about my mum.

"Thanks for the help, and you can stay until the weekend. By then your mum will be back and you should go home, right?"

She doesn't answer me, just turns on her heel and goes into her—my—bedroom.

I go into Mum's room and pick up the notes I've been making about what to do next.

1. *Go to the public library and ask about how to find someone in prison.* Feels very risky.
2. *Go to the council office and find out how much mum owes.* I've been too scared to go all week.
3. *Google prison names again.*
4. *Rob a bank.*
5. *Ask a teacher.* No way. I took Tuesday off to try and get my head together. Then I forged Mum's signature on a sick note. My form teacher tossed it to one side. They've got an inspection coming up, and everyone seems to scream at everyone else.
6. *Ask Jordan, ask his parents, ask Tasha's mum, ask Dom's mum.*

I scratch out number 6 so hard I almost rip the paper. I can't ask *anyone.*

For the first time in my life I've got a proper friend/boyfriend and there's someone my age sleeping over in the house, even though she's the most annoying person in the world. But I'm totally miserable.

Right now I'd give anything to go back to it being just Mum, me and the collection. This is the first time we've ever been away from each other. I've never been on school trips. I've never been invited for a sleepover. It feels so horrible without her all the time.

Every time I try to imagine Jordan coming to my house, I want to vomit. His home is so beautiful and he's so immaculate, streaking down the pool, his golden body scrubbed, nails so clean and neat. Fastidious swim champ Jordan Prince would totally lose interest in pathetic Josie Tate if he knew the truth.

Tasha and Dom have probably realized this, I suddenly think, and a chill goes through me. If I chuck Tasha out, what's to stop them from telling Jordan? They know where we'll be on Saturday night. I can't trust them, not if Tasha's desperate. Desperate people do bad things.

I'm trapped. I have to let Tasha stay and even let her have Dom over. Otherwise I might as well text Jordan now and say I'm not coming. A feeling of despair washes over me. Who am I kidding, thinking I can keep all this secret from him?

My fingers hover over the keys on my mobile. I should text him right now, but then I think of his cool palm on the back of my head as he helps me float. I love being in the water with Jordan. The pool's like another home to him, maybe the one where he feels the most comfortable. As he streaks down his short course, racing the clock, there's no place like that for Jordan Prince.

I can't break it off, I tell myself.

But before I fall asleep I decide I'll go to the council office after my paper route and write myself a fake note for the dentist. I don't think anyone at school will care right now if I'm missing for a couple of hours. At least I can try to sort out Mum's debt, even if I can't actually find out where she is.

I sleep better than I have all week. The next morning is sunny and warm. Outside the leaves are swirling as I walk past the little park at the end of our road. I feel full of energy and whip around with the papers. When I've finished, I have a tea and a bacon roll in Terry's, and then I catch the bus to the council offices near the pool.

I'm not going to shower until later because I don't want to bump into Jordan. The next time he sees me I'm going to be the new, made-over Josie Tate, and his face will light up like in the films. But I can't help feeling nervous at the thought of Dom's beauty-expert cousin. She'll probably take one look at my shaggy hair and refuse to touch it.

The bus arrives dead on nine. I can see someone already going into the offices.

I take a deep breath and smooth down my hair and my clothes. I'm wearing Mum's best coat to look older.

I cross the street, go inside and up to reception. There's a woman sitting there, graying short hair, probably fifty at least, tapping away at a computer.

"Good morning," I say, in my interview-type voice.

The woman doesn't look up.

"I need, I mean, I want to ask something, er, about council tax," I say.

She stops tapping and stares at me, looks me up and down and then jerks her head to the left. "Down that corridor, last room on the right."

I walk down the corridor, my legs wobbling, and go into the room with a label on the door that says ENQUIRIES.

There's no one inside, but there are a couple of chairs and a long desk at the end. I sit on one of the chairs. A big clock on the wall ticks ten minutes by.

I think of Jordan racing up and down the pool and the huge clock with the black hand marking off the seconds, deciding if he wins or loses.

"Sometimes," he said on Tuesday evening, "I feel as if my whole life is divided into single seconds."

The door swings open, and a woman, older than Mel, in a black suit with reddish-brown hair in a gleaming bob, comes in. "Can I help you?"

"Yes," I say, and stand up.

The woman sits down at the desk and looks up at me expectantly.

"I just wanted to inquire about our, my mum's, well our council tax. I think there's been some mistake."

"Name and address?" says the woman, staring at her computer screen.

I give the details and she taps away.

Then she frowns and says, "Your mother is in prison for nonpayment. There's no mistake. Have you come to pay the debt?"

I stare at her, my heart sinking.

"The total is £5,466.42." The woman doesn't even look up.

Thousands and thousands. Oh God! I was right.

"Oh," I say.

"Your mother is out of work, so the council can't garnishee the money from her wages." She taps some more on her keyboard.

That was Len's word, *garnishee,* taking the money from Mum's pay. How can I explain to this woman that my crazy mother is trying to save the planet for all of us? She doesn't even look at me when she speaks.

"I don't know what your mum spends her money on, but she should be paying her bills first," she says. "So if you haven't come to pay the debt, then ask someone else in the family to do so. Otherwise your mother will serve her full sentence."

A mobile sounds off, and the woman pulls it out of her bag and starts a long conversation. I feel as though I've been dismissed from the Head's office.

I walk out of the building and across the road to the pool, go into the changing rooms and sit down. I'm panting as if I've been running. I can hardly catch my breath, I'm so scared.

£5,466.42.

It's a fortune.

I'm going to kill Mum when she comes home!

15.

Saturday morning there's no sign of Jordan when I go to the pool for a shower. Part of me's pleased because my life's getting so muddled, I'm scared I might just blurt out everything to him. But I'm also thinking about tonight. What if he has he gone off to another competition and forgotten about our date?

I catch sight of Chantelle in the canteen and call out, "Has practice been canceled?"

She's sitting with Taylor and the rest of the team. She tosses her ponytail over her shoulder as she looks me up and down.

I feel myself squirm.

"Med check," she says, and turns back to her friends.

What does that mean?

Taylor takes pity on me and says, "We get a monthly check with a doctor, and Jordan's appointment's this morning."

"Oh, sure," I say automatically.

But as I walk off I hear Chantelle snigger, "Does she think she's American or something?"

Low laughter breaks out. I feel myself flush right down the neck.

I take a shower and go off to my paper route, but all the time I'm thinking about what the woman in the council offices said yesterday. I still can't get my head around Mum's debt. It's absolutely massive, and I have no idea how to pay it.

I spent most of last night going through her stuff to see what I could sell. She's got a few pieces of jewelry I could take to the Gold Shack on the High Street. But there's no way they're worth £5,000.00.

I hardly slept for worrying. By morning all I could think was, Poor Mum. She devotes her life to saving the world from drowning in rubbish. Then she ends up in prison and her darling daughter sells off anything she can find.

I feel so guilty.

I'm just finishing my paper route when my phone bleeps. It's a text from Jordan.

Still ok for tonite JP x

X. . . a kiss . . . OMG!! My first-ever virtual kiss. I'm reeling as I stare at the screen, and then I type in my reply. *Can't wait JT xx*

My finger hovers over the delete key, but I press Send. I let out the breath I've been holding for minutes with a big sigh.

My hand's shaking. I've topped him with two kisses back. Is that okay?

I stand outside my front door staring at my phone, and then the bleep sounds like a siren.

Me too xxxx

Yeess!! Four whole kisses!

I leap into the air with both feet and come down laughing out loud. I scroll back through all our texts and stand there on the pavement reading them over and over again. The sun's warm on my face and a bird is singing on a rooftop. I don't have to think about Mum and prison and £5,000.00. I can just be

Josie Tate, a teenage girl in love with swim champ, gorgeous Japanese eyes, American accent, Jordan Prince.

My phone bleeps again, but this time it's Dom and I come back to earth.

meet you at hairdresser 6:30 Dom

I text back and go into the house. It feels so silent, more than I have ever noticed since Mum disappeared. I nearly call out to Tasha, but then I remember she's gone over to Dom's to stay the night there. A chill goes through me. I'll be all alone in the house tonight for the first time. Ever.

I go up to Mum's room, dump my bag and pull open a little drawer in a table next to her bed. This is where she keeps our documents and her jewelry. There's a gold ring with maybe a diamond in it, but I'm not really sure, as well as a couple of gold chains and a thick gold bracelet. There's also a cameo brooch that I think belonged to Grandma Bet.

She died when Mum was eleven, and for the first time I begin to think what that must have been like. My mum's in prison for a few weeks and it feels like forever. Death is properly forever.

Mum said to me once, "When your Grandma Bet died, I didn't get out of bed for a week. My sister was only fourteen. Dad went to the pub every night. Your grandma was the key to our family. After she died, everything fell apart."

I was ten, and Mum had come in to read me a story. My room was quite empty in those days, even though the rest of the house was almost full.

"We'll always be together, Mum, won't we?" I'd said, and patted her hand.

She didn't answer for a minute or two, and my heart was thumping away while I waited. Then she said, "It's years until you're sixteen."

Now as I sit on her bed I wonder if Mum thinks I'll be leaving home at sixteen because that was the age she was when she had to cope by herself. She was pregnant with me, and Grandpa was still alive, but he was so ill he wasn't any help, she told me. Then he died when I was two, and Mum was left totally alone.

How did she manage? I can hardly cope right now. I even miss moany Tasha Brown.

I let out a sigh, empty my wet things onto the bed, sling the jewelry in my bag and go out of the house. I walk to the High Street and into the Gold Shack, open my bag and drop the stuff onto the counter.

There's a Polish guy behind the counter, in his thirties with his head shaved bald. He turns the stuff over a couple of times, gives a shrug, and says, "Hundred."

"Pounds? Is that all? Come on, that's a diamond." My voice is at whine pitch. Get a grip, Josie, I tell myself.

"No diamond, crystal, Czech. No diamond." He's shaking his head firmly.

What do I know? I can't believe anyone in my family had diamonds.

And there's no way Mum could buy a diamond. She's spent all her money for almost her entire life in secondhand shops.

But I'm desperate, and I've got to give it my best. "Two hundred," I say. I'm almost shouting to stop my voice from wobbling. My legs have turned to water. I'm sure he's about to tell me to leave.

He stares hard at me and then he breaks into a grin. He has quite a nice face when he smiles. "I give you one-fifty."

I'm so relieved I want to fist pump the air, but I manage to stay calm and say with a nod, "Deal."

He gives me the money in cash, and I tuck it into my pocket.

As I walk back home I tap the calculator on my phone to see how much I've got:

£87.00 left from the money in Mum's bag

£42.00 savings in my secret biscuit tin

£150.00 from the jewelry

Total = £279.00

Only £5,190.42 to go.

Maybe I should start charging Tasha rent. The thought makes me laugh out loud. A boy going past on his bike yells out, "You're mental!"

I feel mental. I feel as though my life's out of control.

How am I going to get myself together to meet Jordan? I wonder as I let myself in and go upstairs.

For the next couple of hours I poke about in the boxes and sacks in Mum's room, but it's a slow job. I feel like a burglar, or even worse, a policeman looking for evidence. I keep stopping and thinking I can hear her come in. If she saw what I was doing she'd go ballistic.

I don't find anything that remotely looks valuable. I really do wonder at some of the stuff she's collected over the years. There are three sacks of skirts. Who needs so many skirts? Ten boxes are just full with empty plastic bottles. They're going in the recycling bin in the side passage, I decide. Mum would be pleased if I did some proper recycling, wouldn't she?

But I'll do it in the morning. I've done enough damage for one day, I tell myself.

Outside it's been dark for ages. When I check the time it's nearly six, and I'm not even dressed yet. I panic and pull off my T-shirt and jeans and then I can't find my black tights. That takes another five minutes hunting in my room.

Finally, I've got everything on: tights, shorts, top, black

lace-up shoes—I wish I had proper boots like the ones Tasha wears, but these will have to do. I grab my bag, check I have money and keys and dash up to High Street.

I arrive at the hairdresser where Dom's cousin works, ten minutes late, with a red sweaty face and panting hard.

"Where the hell have you been?" snarls Tasha.

"No worries," says Dom in his kind voice. "This is Angel, my cousin."

A tall goddess with jet-black skin, hair slick against her head, pouting red lips and the slimmest legs I've ever seen poured into white jeans is standing in front of a mirror at the far end of the room.

I catch my breath, wipe my forehead with the back of my hand, and say, "Hi, Angel. Thanks so much for, er, doing this."

Angel gives me the same up/down scan as Chantelle, and without moving a muscle in her face, jerks her head toward the sink.

I hesitate, and then Tasha says in her bored voice, "She needs to wash your hair before she can straighten it."

"Oh, sure."

Dom and Tasha settle down in a corner with their mobiles, chatting and laughing as they stare at screens.

Angel washes my hair in shampoo that smells of coconut, dries it with a towel and then spends what seems like hours trimming, combing and then straightening it until it hangs at least three inches shorter in a smooth drop of light brown hair. It looks utterly amazing, but when I say so Angel doesn't even flick her eyes at me.

Then she turns me in the chair, away from the mirror, and applies makeup. When she turns me back to the mirror, I gasp.

Dom comes over and gives a long wolf whistle. "Hey, Josie. You look gorgeous. What do you think, Tasha?"

"Yeah, yeah," says Tasha, flicking her eyes up from the screen for a second and then back down again.

"Brings out those green eyes," says Angel in a low, smooth voice. She looks quite pleased with herself.

I thank her and she says it's nothing; it's good practice for her course. I offer her a ten-pound note, which to my enormous relief she refuses, but I go out of the shop feeling like such a creep.

"Are you sure, Dom?" I say as we walk off.

"Angel's cool. She did it for me."

"You're lucky to have such a great cousin."

"We're a big family," he says. "Eh, Tasha?"

Tasha shrugs and then her face breaks into grin. "Mmmm," she says. "Is that him? He's so fit."

Jordan's standing on the street a few yards ahead. He raises his hand when he sees me.

I didn't want Tasha and Dom to meet him. What if they start talking about my house?

"Hi. We've heard all about you and the swimming," says Tasha, sashaying up to Jordan.

I want to melt through the pavement.

"Uh, right," says Jordan.

"You like live gigs?" says Dom, before I can get a word in edgeways.

Jordan nods and Dom says, "Come over to Shanks tonight, other end of High Street. Me and Tasha follow a band, Rough Steel. It'll be a good night, guaranteed."

Jordan says, "Sure, after we've eaten. Uh, do you wanna join us?"

No way!

But Dom shakes his head, grinning at me and says, "We'll see you later."

As they walk off, Dom's arm round Tasha's shoulders, Jordan says, "Nice pair."

"They're just good friends," I say.

"You sure about that?"

"Course," I say. "Hungry?"

"Starving, and what have you done to your hair?"

"You don't like it?"

"It looks amazing."

Then he takes my arm and steers me into the restaurant.

16.

"I didn't book a table," murmurs Jordan, as he looks around nervously.

"Do you think it matters?"

He shrugs.

I have no idea. Me and Mum only ever go to cheap cafés. A waiter wearing a black T-shirt and blue jeans, with a white cloth over his shoulder, comes over and says, "Hi. You guys ready to eat?"

He has a snub nose and red cheeks that glow as he grins at us. I feel myself relax. Jordan nods, still looking quite spooked.

So I say, "Let's sit in a booth."

We slide onto the red plastic seats opposite each other, and the waiter gives the table a quick wipe with his cloth. Then he plops down two huge menus and leaves us to it.

Jordan's staring at me. "First time I've seen you in makeup."

I go red and mutter, "Yes."

"It's kinda nice. Did you cut your hair?"

"A bit."

He nods. "Fit better under your swim cap."

"Is that all you ever think about?"

I mean it as a joke, but it comes out all wrong, and his eyes sink back into their sockets.

"Pretty much," he says.

I have no idea what else to say. What do you talk about on a date? I almost wish Crystal was here, or Hugo picking up his sushi rolls with his fingers and laughing away. They'd know what to talk about.

We both read the menu for ages.

Then Jordan says, "Shall I order wine?"

My eyes open wide with amazement and we stare at each other. Then I can't help it. This enormous giggle bursts up through me, and we both start laughing so much Jordan drops his menu. When he bends down to pick it up, he sweeps his cutlery off the table too, and I laugh even harder.

"What?" he says.

"It's a burger place, not the Hilton."

"But that's what my dad always says to my mom when he takes us out for dinner."

His eyes are crinkled into a smile. I smile back, and for a moment we just sit there, grinning at each other. Then I say, "We're stupid teenagers, and I'm having a chocolate milkshake, okay?"

"Cool, we'll make that two. How about the Texan—looks like the biggest burger, with skin-on fries and onion rings?"

"Excellent choice," I say in a posh accent, and we both giggle again.

The waiter comes back and says, "You guys having fun?"

He takes our order, nods with approval and disappears.

We're silent again. When the milkshakes appear we both sit for ages sucking through the straw, trying to make as little noise as possible. Halfway through Jordan come up for air, fumbles in the top pocket of his jean jacket and pulls out a small rectangular parcel. He hands it to me silently.

"What's this?" I say. A little thrill goes through me.

"Open it."

It's beautifully wrapped in gold paper with a gold ribbon. I pull the ribbon gently, then slide my fingernail under the tape, terrified I'll rip the paper. Inside is a white box with CALVIN KLEIN BEAUTY on the side.

Jordan's bought me perfume on our first date.

I stare at it for ages until Jordan says, "Crystal thought it would be good. But I can always take it back. . . ."

"No, I mean, yes—well, I've never had perfume before." I stop and blush, I feel so dumb.

"Try it, see if you like it."

I open the box and slide out the bottle. Then I unscrew the top and smell it. It's heavenly.

I dab some behind my ears like I've seen Mum do, and then on the inside of each wrist. Then I hold out my wrist and say, "What do you think?"

He takes my hand. His skin feels so soft and gentle, and then he leans forward and sniffs. "Nice," he says. "Everyone on the team wears something. Takes away the smell of pool water."

"What about you?"

"Hugo Boss."

I have no idea what that smells like. I'm just planning to go and investigate next time I'm on the High Street when he leans forward, turning his head to one side, and says, "What do you think?"

His cheek's so close I almost kiss it but instead I sniff and say, "Wonderful."

As he leans back the food arrives, and the burgers are enormous, just like Dom said.

"Enjoy your meal," says the cheery waiter.

The music changes on the speakers, and Jordan says, "The Eagles, Dad's favorite band."

"Great sound," I say.

Then we attack the food and every single mouthful is so delicious, almost as good as Nariko's dinner last week.

The food seems to push a button in Jordan. Between mouthfuls he starts speaking about his hopes for an Olympic Gold one day and how lonely training can be. "Dad gets it, but Mom, she doesn't understand. She thinks I'll grow out of it. I mean, how dumb can you be?"

His eyebrows shoot up in amazement, and I nod and grin through a mouthful of burger.

"Dad's always said I should follow my dream. He's the one who taught me to swim. I was spotted by a coach when I was in grade school. Mom thinks I should study much harder, but what's the point if you're no good at exams?"

"I can see the problem," I say, dipping my chips in barbecue sauce.

"So I never complain at home."

"About what?"

"Uh, you know, not being invited to parties, not having girlfriends." He stops and stares at me. "I've tried asking girls out, but they don't understand that my swimming comes first. You're the first person who gets it."

I stop eating and swirl my straw around in the glass. Then I say, "My life's not that straightforward, so who am I to judge?"

"So tell me, Josie. I don't know anything; you won't even let me come to your house."

His eyes are fixed on me now with such an intense look, I duck my head. Then I say, "Oh, there's nothing much to tell. I live with my mum. Dad disappeared before I was born. No brothers and sisters or anyone else. We live in a boring house near the park. My mum is a very private person, so she doesn't like people coming by."

"Sure," he says. "That's okay. What does she do?"

I think for a minute and then I say, "She's in recycling. My mum believes that every single person should do their best to save the planet from dying under a mound of stuff."

"She has strong principles."

I nod. He's right. That's Mum exactly, only look where it landed her—prison. "So, I don't really have friends either."

He looks at me with disbelief. "Are you kidding me? You're such a great person. What's the problem?"

I feel flustered and dive under the table to look for my napkin. When I come up there's something in my eye, and I mutter about finding the loo. Jordan stands up as I go. I hurry through the restaurant wondering what I should say to him.

In the loo it looks like some of my eye makeup has smudged. I get a tissue and dab away at it, but that just makes it worse and now I look like a panda. Red with embarrassment I wend my way back to our table, a tissue over my eye.

"You okay? Let me take a look."

Jordan reaches a hand up to my eye and takes away the tissue. His face is so close we are literally staring into each other's eyes. We stay like that for what seems ages.

Then he leans back and I say, "My makeup's smudged. I didn't put it on—it was a cousin of Dom's and I look stupid now."

"No way. You'd never look stupid, Josie. You don't need makeup. You have such beautiful green eyes, like the sea. I like you just normal."

I smile and say, "Only with Calvin Klein perfume."

He shrugs. "If you like."

Then he looks at his watch and says, "You want to go to the gig still?"

I don't but I say, "Do you?"

"Oh sure, I love live music."

"Me too."

He gives me a huge grin and pays the bill. We walk off, hand in hand.

I feel as though I'm streaking down the pool, floating on air. Jordan's humming a tune from one of his favorite bands, so I think he feels the same.

I've never been so happy in all my life. Have I?

17. Tasha

"Why did you invite them?" I hiss to Dom, as we walk away from Jordan and Josie.

"Because you need Josie for the sleepovers, don't you?" says Dom in a quiet voice.

I jerk around to look at him, and he stares back with his steady brown eyes. That strange flutter washes through my stomach again.

"Want to tell me what's going on?" he says.

We walk on down the road. I snuggle closer as he tightens his arm round my waist and give a little laugh. "Nothing's going on, you muppet."

"But you don't want to sleep at home, do you? Why not?"

I knew he wouldn't give up, but I've had time to get my story straight. "Okay, okay, it's silly really. Had a big row with Mum and I just need a bit of space."

"About what?"

"Money," I say, really quickly.

Dom knows that's something me and Mum often fall out over, but I'm not sure he's convinced yet.

"So why are you wearing purple?"

I glance down at the skirt I pulled out of a sack in Josie's house. I had to find something to wear tonight, but Dom knows I hate purple, and the skirt's too long.

I give a girly giggle and say, "I love purple."

Dom raises his eyebrows, and I know he's going to take some convincing.

I giggle again and say, "A girl can change her mind, can't she?"

"Women," he says with a snort.

But I can see that I'm getting somewhere, so I say, "Got any booze with you?"

He can't help grinning and says, "As if."

We walk on past a bus stop and we're nearly at Shanks. There's a crowd of kids up ahead going in the same direction.

Everyone loves Rory, I think with an inward sigh. But maybe tonight's the night he asks me out on a proper date. I even begin to wonder if I should just march up to him and tell him I'm in love with him. We could go out after the gig. Dom can call his dad for a lift home; I'm sure Rory would make sure I get home safe to Josie's.

I can't help wondering if Dom would actually say anything if I went off with Rory. Then a voice breaks into my thoughts.

"Tasha! Yoo-hoo, over here!"

It's Mum. She's hanging off Chaz's shoulder. Chaz is already leering at me, and they both look drunk. Dom stiffens and a sudden terror goes through me that he's going to ask Mum about all the sleepovers. Somehow I've got to stop them.

"Hey, Mum. Where're you off to?" I call out, slapping a grin on my face and trying not to meet Chaz's eye.

"Curry. Just had a few beers, you know." Her speech is slurred. "Nice to see you, Dom. How's your mum?"

"Fine, thanks, Mrs. Brown," says Dom. He's eyeing Chaz up and down.

There's a few seconds when no one knows what to say. Then in one swift movement, Chaz pulls a twenty-pound note out of his pocket and stuffs it down my top.

I gasp and Dom takes a step forward, but Chaz pulls Mum past us and calls out, "Have a good night on me, kids. See you later."

Then they disappear into The Curry House.

"Who's that?" asks Dom.

"Mum's boyfriend, Chaz."

"Does he often give you money, Tash?"

"No!"

I pull the money out of my top, rip it into tiny pieces and stuff the bits down a drain in the gutter.

"Satisfied?"

Dom has a startled, puzzled look on his face. He thinks he knows about my life, but actually he doesn't know anything. There's nothing he can do about Chaz, so what's the point of telling him? I realize for the first time how desperately alone I am. No family, no friends I can trust, not even my sweet little Dom.

"Oh, come on," I say impatiently. I tug him toward the entrance to Shanks. "Let's get off our heads."

He hesitates and then gives a little grin.

Inside, the room's packed and pumping. Rory's thrown his head back, and he's uprooted the entire mike stand as he struts across the tiny stage. Everyone's jumping up and down, rocking to the music.

It's like we all fall into a trance as Rory settles down into a steady chant, over and over, *It's just my angel storm. It's just my angel storm*. I throw my arms around Dom's neck, looming over him. We sway, eyes closed.

I so wish I was in Rory's arms as I sing the words in Dom's ear. But it's Dom who's here with me right now, and his body is so, well, familiar—always warm with its cinnamon and clean-wash scent.

"You're just my angel storm," he sings in my ear, and we giggle together.

My sweet little Dom. Will he always stick by me, no matter what happens with Mum and Chaz?

Someone taps my shoulder. It's one of the girls from school. She's got a half-bottle of vodka. We pass it between us until the end of the song. My head is spinning, and Dom's begging in my ear, "Enough, Tash. Don't drink anymore, please."

But I don't care about anything or anyone tonight. No one cares about me. No one has space for me, and it's all because of Chaz. No one understands. I don't even understand.

I want more drink. I want to lose my mind in this pumping room, and then I'm going to grab Rory and *make* him love me. Maybe that's the only way you really get love—you grab it and punch it and push it until the other person gives in. Is that what Chaz wants?

"Tash!" It's Josie, and Jordan's wrapped around her shoulders. They look *so* happy. I hate them!

Jordan offers me a beer, and I take it before Dom can say no. I glug down half before I come up for breath. Jordan laughs as the entire room sways and then uprights itself.

"Whoo-hoo, man!" I croak.

"You know how to party," says Jordan, grinning at me.

But Josie's frowning. How dare she! Josie with the hoarder,

psycho mum. Does she think she's better than off-her-head, miserable Tasha Brown?

We dance and dance. Somehow I manage to get my mouth around two more bottles of vodka and take quite a few swigs. All my limbs are floppy, my arms flying everywhere. I bang one guy in his glasses.

"You muppet!" I shout, as Dom apologizes for me. My voice sounds slurred, just like Mum and Chaz.

I see Dom leaning toward Jordan and Josie, the two perfect J's. They know where they're sleeping tonight; they have homes. Even a hoarder home is better than no home.

Then Dom is pulling me toward the door. I can feel the other two behind me, guiding me forward. Then we're out in the cold night air, and I'm gasping.

I fling my arms around Dom's neck and say in a slurred voice, "You're always my sweet little Dom, aren't you?"

I can't really see anything clearly. Someone bends my head down and gently pushes me into a car. I hear Josie say, "We can't afford cabs."

"My treat," says Jordan. "We can't leave her like this. Where to?"

Dom gives my address and suddenly I'm screaming, "NO! No! No! Don't take me home." I'm sobbing and sobbing in Dom's arms.

He's soothing me and saying Mum will take care of me. "She won't want you wandering around like this, Tish Tash!"

But I scream so loud the cab driver screeches to a halt. I think Jordan offers him more money because he carries on.

Dom puts his hands on my cheeks and says, "What is it, Tash? What are you so afraid of?"

I shake him away and cry all the way to Josie's front door.

Everyone is out on the street and Dom says, "Tell me, tell me now. I can fix it, Tasha. I can fix anything—you know I can."

It's so cold outside and it's started to rain. All I want to do is get into Josie's bed with Mickey and pull the duvet over my head.

I sway and Dom grabs me. Then suddenly everything pours out. My voice slurs as I say, between sobs, "I can't go home because Chaz's been perving on me in the shower and coming into my room when I'm undressed and giving me money and he says he wants to..."

"He WHAT?"

There's a huge crash as Dom karate-kicks a beer bottle on the curb. It shatters all over the pavement. I stumble away from him as a sound comes from his mouth like nothing I've ever heard before. Jordan and Josie have shrunk away against the wall.

"I'll KILL him!" shrieks Dom. "I'll RIP him open! I'll pull his fingers off one by one! The bastard! He's so dead! I swear. He'll NEVER go near you...."

Jordan grabs him as a police car turns into the top of the street and begins a slow crawl toward us. "Shut up, Dom! They'll arrest you."

Dom's mouth seems locked open but he stops his rant, and Josie quickly opens the front door. Everyone piles inside.

18. Josie

I'm so busted.

Everyone's in the hallway, crushed together because there's only a tiny space between all the stuff piled to the ceiling. I glance over my shoulder and see Tasha slumped all over Dom, who's still snorting like a caged animal.

Jordan's the last one inside and pulls the front door shut. Then he turns. The look on his face sends a shiver right through me.

I am totally dumped, I know it.

"Dom needs a hot drink after shouting like that," says Tasha, her voice still slurred. "There's a kettle upstairs. Lead on, Josie, babes."

I could kill her! I try to catch her eye, but she's looking down.

"Uh, Jordan, maybe you could catch up with that taxi now and go home," I say. My voice is almost at whine pitch. "You don't want to be late for training."

Jordan shrugs. Tasha gives me a prod.

"Come *on*," she says with a groan. "I'm desperate for a pee."

I don't want to make a scene. There's nothing for it but to

squeeze down the hallway, everyone following behind me, tears welling in my eyes.

Upstairs Tasha pushes past me with Dom and goes into Mum's room. I can hear her fussing around with the kettle. I'm left on the landing with Jordan, hands in his pockets, shoulders drooped, as he stares through the open door of the bathroom.

I think of his beautiful home, his mum's white carpet, everyone taking their shoes off and not a speck of dust anywhere. His competition cups gleaming and all that wonderful food his mum cooks. Jordan's seen our kitchen stuffed to the door *and* the bathroom *and* Mum's bedroom. Now he knows all my secrets.

"You got a lot of stuff," he says, his voice dry and croaky.

"Mum's a collector," I say, but it sounds so lame.

He gives me a quizzical look.

I try again. "She recycles because everyone throws so much stuff away and its all, well, useful. . . ."

He looks up and down the landing again and then he says, "Sure." But his voice is very faint.

He's horrified, I think, his hands deep in his pockets so that he doesn't get contaminated by our house. I stare at the floor, wishing I'd never met him. Then I would never have had any hope of love or friendship or any of those things.

For years I've been planning to have one good clear-up. It would only take a weekend, I'm positive.

But Mum never agreed, did she? Now she's gone and I'm left with a houseful of so-called friends, one of whom has nearly drunk herself to death because of her mum's boyfriend, and that's awful. But is it as bad as my life?

My head's spinning, so I say, "Poor Tash."

"Yes," says Jordan quickly, and I can see he's relieved to focus on something else. "She should go to the police."

"She's been staying with me since the storm last Monday. I couldn't understand why she didn't go home. . . ."

"Now you get it, Josie, babes," Tasha calls out from the bedroom.

Jordan and I stare at each other, and I say, "What's your mum doing about it?"

"She won't listen," says Tasha in a miserable voice. "She says it's all *my* fault."

Dom snorts loudly and says, "Wait till I tell my mum. She'll go over and sort it out, Tash, don't you worry."

Tasha just gives a grim laugh. I make a move toward the stairs, nodding to Jordan to follow. He nods back and starts forward, bumping into a pile of boxes.

"Sorry," he says.

I want to die. We carry on more slowly, but before we get back to the stairs, a huge thumping breaks out on the front door.

We freeze and Jordan's eyes widen as he raises an eyebrow toward me. I shake my head and shrug. I glance at my watch. It's after eleven.

The thumping stops and a voice yells out, "Come on, open up! Freezing out here."

It's a man's voice.

Dom has come out into the corridor and suddenly he pushes past us, grabbing a golf club from the bathroom doorway. Then he's rushing down the stairs, brandishing it, yelling, "It's that bastard, Chaz! I'm going to kill him!"

Tasha's screaming behind me. Jordan shoves me out the way, leaping behind Dom, yelling, "C'mon man, it's not worth it!"

He just manages to grab Dom before he reaches the front

door. He's bigger and stronger than little Dom, but there's still a terrible struggle until Dom subsides, panting. Jordan wrenches the golf club out of his hand. We all stand behind the door, listening.

There's a silence and then a woman's voice says quite gently, "We're looking for Josie. Got a letter from her mum. Are you in there, darling?"

"Where's your mum gone?" whispers Jordan.

"It's not Chaz," hisses Tasha to Dom.

"You can trust us, Josie. We know your mum. Elaine Tate, innit? She told us to come special to see you, give you her letter. I met her last week in the prison just before I come out."

Tasha lets out a gasp and Jordan throws me such a shocked look that morphs into total disgust.

We're finished.

I push past everyone and open the front door. My body feels as though gravity's pulling it through the pavement into the molten center of the earth.

Outside is a woman, older than Mum, maybe forties, with spiky white-blond hair, rings through her eyebrows and nose and three studs above her lip. She's about my height but very broad. She's wearing a tight leather jacket, jeans and scruffy suede ankle boots stained along the toes. Her mouth's smiling but her eyes are flat and gray. She's holding up an envelope, but all I can think is how podgy her fingers look, with rings jammed on each one, even the thumb.

Her voice, though sharp-edged, is still quite gentle as she says, "You're so like her, Josie, same green eyes. I told you, Bazza, didn't I?"

She looks at the man next to her, who's even older, with shoulder-length, greasy hair and white sideburns. He's very thin, with droopy shoulders, a cigarette tucked behind his ear and nicotine-stained fingers.

"I said they'd have the same eyes," the woman went on. "Got your friends here, have you, darling?"

"We going in, Shirl?" says the man in a monotone.

I feel a movement behind me. It's Jordan. He squeezes past me and onto the pavement. He's still got his hands in his pockets, and I think he's going to walk off without saying anything.

But he turns and there's such a look of disappointment in his eyes. They've shrunk so far back into the sockets, they're like thin lines beneath his beautiful thick eyebrows.

"I have to go," he says, and he looks past me to Dom, gives him a swift nod and walks away.

Forever? I wonder.

Maybe that's the best thing, I tell myself, and I feel such a pain in my chest I think I'm going to stop breathing.

"Put the kettle on, girly," Shirl says, breaking into my thoughts. "We're dying for a cuppa, innit?"

Then everyone's inside again, only minus Jordan and plus Shirl and Bazza. They both smell of stale cigarette smoke and beer. They're pushing us forward, muttering to each other about the state of the house. I realize I don't care anymore who sees our house and what they think about it. It's just a place to sit and wait for Mum to come home. Then I remember the letter.

"Can I have the letter, please?" I say, turning around on the stairs and reaching my hand out to Shirl.

She gives me a steady look and passes it up to me.

The envelope's creased and it looks as if it's been opened.

"I managed to smuggle it out so they don't read it in the prison," says Shirl. "That's what your mum wanted. No privacy in prison, innit?"

I bet you've read it, I think, but I don't say anything. I don't like these two. They're criminals, aren't they? What have they done, murdered people or mugged them or robbed banks? My mum's not like that. She's in debt, not dangerous.

I don't trust them but I need to hear what they have to say because Mum hasn't rung since that first call.

So I paste a smile on my face and take them into Mum's room. Bazza settles himself on the bed first, propped up against all of Mum's pillows, and Shirl drops down beside him. They look as though they own the place. Tasha and Dom are still downstairs.

I pick up the kettle. "I'll just go and fill it," I say.

"You do that, girly," says Shirl, with her strange smiling lips and blank eyes. Then she puts a cigarette in her mouth and says to Bazza, "Got a light?"

"Oh, Mum says no smoking in the house," I say quickly.

But they ignore me and settle back, puffing away contentedly.

I go into the bathroom, shaking with anger, turn the tap on and sit down on the loo. Then I open the envelope and pull out the letter.

Dear Josie,

I am so so so sorry. I never thought they would send me to prison. I made up a story about you going to live with your Aunty Mary in Hull so that they wouldn't come and take you into care. I know you can manage by yourself. I've had to write this really quickly so Shirl can hide it into her bra and smuggle it out. Listen, Josie. Your Grandpa Ted left you

some money in a building society account. It
was supposed to be for when you go to college.
But somehow the account book got lost in the
collection over the years. I know I put it inside
a pink makeup bag, but no idea where it is.
If you have a bit of a sort-out, you'll find it.
There's thousands in there, Josie. You could
pay the debt and get me out of prison. Shirl
will help you, she's been a good friend to me
this week. We shared a cell and she helped me
learn the ropes, kept me safe. When you find
the money, go to the building society and get
it out. Find it soon and get me out, Josie. I
can't stand it without my beautiful collection
around me. It's horrible in here.

I miss you so much and I love you,
Mum xxx

I read the letter twice more. She says she misses me, but really it's her stupid collection she's missing. She can't stand being separated from it. That's the very same collection that swallows all of Mum's money so that she doesn't even buy me food, let alone pay her stupid bills.

"Josie!" It's Shirl calling me.

I don't answer. I put the letter away in my jeans pocket and fill up the kettle. If Shirl and Bazza have read this letter, then they know about the money. Will they try to steal it from me?

As I go down the corridor, Tasha appears at the top of the stairs. She puts her finger to her lips to stop me from calling out.

I go over and she whispers, "Dom's gone. His mum phoned. She's not well and his dad's working nights. He has to help with his brothers. Now what?"

"I don't know how to get rid of them," I whisper back.

We stare at each other, and in that moment everything between us changes. Tasha with the mum who doesn't protect her and me with the mum in prison, neither of us with a proper home. We're going to face this together, I think. I give her a firm nod. She nods back and then we go into Mum's room.

"Took your time," growls Bazza.

But Shirl gives her creepy grin and says, "Don't mind him, grumpy old sod. So what's your name, girly? Milk, two sugars for us, Josie."

"I'm Tasha, I'm staying with Josie while my mum's in Spain, and we don't keep milk in the house. Plenty of sugar though."

Tasha's voice is sharp as barbed wire, and there's no sign of being drunk now. I pour the tea and hand it around.

"So what prison did you say you were in with my mum?" I say casually, leaning against a pile of boxes.

"I didn't," says Shirl, eyeing me up and down. "But it's Fenton, about ten miles from here. What do you think, Bazza?"

"Yep, ten mile or so."

"When's visiting time?" I say.

"It ain't like a hospital, girly," says Shirl. "You have to get permission, and you're under sixteen, ain't you? You need a relative to ask for you."

My heart sinks. There's no one I can ask without them knowing I'm home alone.

Tasha gives me a sympathetic look and squeezes my arm. Then she stretches and yawns, saying, "I need to crash. Lot of homework to do in the morning."

I take the hint and say, "Me too."

I stare at Shirl and Bazza, willing them to go.

As if she can read my mind, Shirl says in a lazy voice, "Your mum said we could stay a couple of days, just until we get on our feet, innit."

So that's their plan, and there's nothing I can do.

Tasha pulls my arm and we go out and down to my room. I slump onto my narrow single bed. "Where are we going to sleep?"

Tasha's surprisingly practical and soon we're in bed, top to tail and at least it's warm. Then I tell her about the letter.

"So that's why they're here," she says. "They've come for the money, Josie. We've got to outwit those two or they'll bleed you dry, and you'll never get your mum out of prison."

That's what I'm terrified of, I think just before I fall asleep with Tasha Brown's toenails jammed against my leg. How much lower is my life going to sink? And will I ever see Jordan again?

JP and JT forever. Ha-ha.

19. Tasha

Tasha's Vlog
Sunday, October 20, 8:45 a.m.
I'm sitting in the park at the end of Josie's road and managed to hook onto someone's wifi in the houses nearby. It's cold and damp out here, but I can't vlog in the house anymore—not since those ex-cons moved in. I don't know what Josie's going to do about them. When I went out they were nosing around the boxes in the bathroom. They're gonna fleece her clean, I know they will.

Trouble is, she's too scared to go to the police because they'll put her in care, and I told her I was scared of the same thing. I rang Dom late last night to stop him telling his mum about Chaz. I had to threaten never to speak to him again before he agreed. Josie said something weird when I came off the phone. About Dom really liking me. I told her we've been bezzie mates forever and I'm in love with Rory.

Josie left at half past six for her paper route. We had to sleep in the same bed last night and we both woke soon after five. It was so cold we lay there talking for ages. I really get her now. I feel a bit ashamed about the way I've treated her. She's been a good mate to me, especially since she found out about Chaz. And look at the mess she's in because of her mum. That's totally crazy weird.

She still won't admit her mum's an obsessive mad hoarder, but she told me how she's never had a friend over and never had a boyfriend because she's so ashamed of the way they live. She's a really lonely person. I wouldn't have understood before I had to leave home and everyone abandoned me.

She thinks Jordan has finished with her since he's seen her house, but I told her that's stupid; if he likes her he won't be bothered. She said I was wrong and naive. Me?

I don't want to go back to the house on my own, so Josie said to meet in Terry's at nine and we'll have breakfast and make a plan. I didn't eat anything yesterday and my head's thumping with a massive hangover. I have to stop drinking. If I become an alkie I'll end up living on the streets in a cardboard box, and that's the worst thought in the entire universe.

So...

puts right hand over heart

I promise never to drink again. Now it's on the vlog, it's recorded forever.

I press Stop.

An old man going past with his dog on a leash gives me a strange look. I poke my tongue out at him. He grunts and walks on quickly. Probably thinks I'm a gangsta's girl or something, I look such a state. My hair's all limp and greasy, my clothes are crumpled and there's a dark brown stain on my top. I haven't changed since yesterday evening, and I haven't showered since Friday.

I put my laptop away. It needs charging, and I'm hoping Terry will let me plug it in somewhere. I need one of those posh cafés on the High Street with plugs and wifi, but I can't afford the coffee. For a minute I regret ripping up Chaz's money. Then I shake my head. I'd rather starve.

Josie's already at the counter waiting to be served when I arrive at Terry's.

"Full English?" she says.

"I'm skint."

"We're in this together now," she says in a conspiratorial tone. "Mum left me some money."

"Thanks." I nod and give her a full-on grin. Suddenly I'm not alone anymore. At least Dom knows what my problem is and so does Josie. Maybe between us we can work out how to get rid of Chaz. I mean, how hard can it be?

"You seeing Dom today?" says Josie once we've sat down.

"He has midterm exams soon, so he has to study."

"But we don't have exams this term."

"Dom's like really, really clever. He's doing A Levels next summer. . . ."

"What? Is he sixteen yet?"

"December. He's years ahead of everyone else. What about you? Heard from Jordan?"

Josie shakes her head. "Too scared to text him and he's in training every morning. I thought I'd wait and see if he, you know…"

I nod. "I'm sure he will. He's so into you."

"Do you really think so?" She gives me such a pleading look.

I lay it on thick. "God yes, he didn't take his eyes off you all night. He's smitten, trust me. I know all about love."

I hope I'm right. He didn't look very happy when the ex-cons turned up. Can't blame him really. They scared the hell out of me.

But Josie's soaking all this up. She flashes a real girly smile and flutters her eyelashes a bit. I've never seen her like this.

"I so hope you're right," she gushes. "He's my very first boyfriend. That probably sounds dead stupid to you. But I've never… Well, anyway, he's so gorgeous. I think he's been really lonely, like me, because of always having to train…."

She runs on for ages, and then she stops for a sip of tea.

"You know Dom's totally into you, Tasha. It's like *so* obvious. Even Jordan can see it."

I let out a blast of laughter. "Now who's the naive one? Dom's so young, he's never even thought about girlfriends. You remember Rory last night?"

She grins and says, "The hot lead singer? Who could forget."

"Hands off—he's mine. He dedicated a song to me a while ago. I expect he'll ask me out sometime very soon."

I don't feel all that sure, but he definitely looked at me last night more than once before I got totally hammered.

"Nice," says Josie with an appreciative grin. "He must be nineteen."

"Twenty."

"And definitely luscious. Good luck with it. But be kind to your sweet little Dom."

We have a bit of a laugh. She's all right, is Josie Tate.

We finish breakfast, and then Josie says, "Showers?"

"Definitely."

She's been looking anxiously at her watch. "Jordan will be in the gym for the next two hours," she says, "so we can go to the pool."

We go home to get our stuff and try to sneak past Josie's mum's door, but Shirl calls out, "All right, girls?"

Josie puts her head around and mutters, "Just going out to the library to study."

"Laters, all right?"

Josie gives a grunt and comes out again giving me a look. We exchange raised eyebrows, go and grab our stuff and get out of the house.

All the way to the pool we talk about how to get rid of them, but neither of us can think of a plan beyond poisoning their tea and making them so ill they'd need an ambulance.

"What with? They'd taste bleach or something, wouldn't they?" says Josie.

"I bet Dom has a cousin who'd know how," I say.

"You could ask him."

She's silent then until we get to the changing rooms, and then she says, "What about going home, Tasha? How are we going to get rid of Chaz?"

My eyes suddenly well up and tears are lashing down my cheeks. Josie puts her arms around me. I sob and sob like a little kid. She's warmer than Mickey, who's been almost drowned in my tears in the last week. And she says all the right things, which Mickey can't do.

"I promise, Tasha, we'll get this sorted; we're in this together, right?"

I stop crying and nod.

Then we have the most blissful hot shower of my life, passing the shampoo and shower gel underneath the cubicles to each other and singing "Angel Storm" at the tops of our voices. Josie has a great voice. She can hit the high notes better than Rory... until some old woman yells at us to shut up.

We come out wrapped in towels, our hair dripping all over the floor, bumping shoulders and giggling all the way back to the changing room. Josie shows me how to dry my hair with the hand dryer. I straighten hers as best I can with my hairbrush while she dries it.

"That looks great. Thanks, Tash," she says, all pink and glowing as she stares at herself in the mirror. "Almost as good as Angel did."

"Angel Storm?"

Josie laughs out loud. "We could rename her."

"Here." I pull out my makeup bag, and even though I make it a total rule never to share, I put some lip gloss and eye stuff onto Josie.

"That's great, Tash," she says, and then she holds out a tiny bottle to me. "Here, try this."

"Calvin Klein! That's, like, so expensive." I dab some on my wrists and neck.

"Jordan gave it to me last night, my very first perfume and my very first present from a boy."

Her eyes well up, and she dabs them on a towel.

"See?" I say, putting on eyeliner in front of the mirror. "He's really into you, spending all his money on you."

Josie's quiet for a bit as she gets dressed, and then she says, "So how much do you spend on makeup?"

"About thirty quid a month."

"Wow! It takes me nearly two weeks' work to earn that."

"You earn loads, Josie. Haven't you saved anything? It could pay your mum's debt."

Her head ducks as she starts to pack her things away.

"Sorry," I say. "Don't mean to be nosy."

"No, you're okay," she says in a sad voice. "I need all my money for school stuff, even bits of uniform. My school shoes have holes. And food..." Her voice trails away and she stares at me. Then she continues, "I realize now that my mum spends all her money on her collection. Has done for years. I used to think she was just forgetful about food and clothes and stationery and stuff. But the truth is, she only thinks about one thing: buying everything she sees every single day. She lost her job months ago and stopped paying her council tax. That's why they put her in prison."

She slings her bag on her shoulder, and we walk out of the pool to the bus stop in silence. Rain is falling, and we huddle under a tree, water dripping down the back of my neck.

Then I swing around and grab Josie and say, "We're going to find that money before those criminals do, right Josie?"

I hold my fist out and she stares at it. I grab her hand, bunch her fingers into a fist and bump her.

Her face splits into a grin and she says, "Oh, I get it. Fist bump."

"Deal?" I say.

"Sure."

I think she gets that from Jordan with his American accent.

I so hope he hasn't dumped her. We have enough problems to solve right now.

20. Josie

When we get back to the house and let ourselves in, that eerie silence has descended again. We go upstairs almost on tiptoe, but Mum's room is empty.

"Where are they?" I say.

Tasha shrugs and goes down to my room, but that's empty too.

"Yaaay!" she cries out, fist pumping the air. "They've disappeared."

"We don't know that," I say. "Maybe they went out to eat, like us."

"Do you have a chain on your door?"

"Yes! I'll put it on."

I run downstairs and rush to the front door and ram the chain in place. Then I have an awful thought and rush back to Tasha. "What if they've already found the money and run off?"

Tasha frowns and goes back down to Mum's room. "Look," she says, staring at the bed. "Their bags are still here, and there's a full pack of cigarettes. Can't see Bazza leaving his smokes behind."

I nod.

"And," Tasha goes on, "it doesn't look like they've been rummaging around much."

"Okay," I say. "Well, I'm going to start in the living room. We haven't even opened the door in years. If that bankbook got lost after Grandpa died, then it's more likely to be buried in there than anywhere else. We only stopped using the bathroom two years ago and the kitchen when I was ten. But I can't really remember going into the living room.

"Sounds like a plan," says Tasha.

But before we can make a move Tasha's phone goes. She stares at the screen and then puts the phone to her ear and says, "Yeah?" in a bored voice.

I'm certain it's her mum. I give her a little encouraging nod.

"Why?" Tasha says. "No... nothing much. I'm out of money, what do you expect?... He's definitely away now?... When's he back? Absolutely certain? Because I'm not... Okay, okay. Give me half an hour."

She clicks off and gives a sigh. "Mum's decided she's worried about me. Finally. She wants me to go over there and see if we can make up."

"What do you want to do?"

She eyes me for a moment and then she says, "I need some fresh clothes and some money. But I don't trust her." She breaks off, and her eyes well up.

"You can come back here and stay as long as you like," I say.

Anyway, I'm totally terrified of being left along with Shirl and Bazza.

"Okay," she says slowly. "If I can persuade her to throw that perv out, then you can stay at mine. We can come here every day and look for the money, but you can't stay here on your own any longer."

I must admit that's a big relief, and we hug. She grabs her bag and disappears out the front door. I put the chain back on and then tackle the living room.

The door opens such a tiny crack when I push it, I can only get my hand and arm inside. But I grab a small bag and pull it through, and then another, until I have eased the door enough to get inside. It's unbelievable. The stuff is piled through the entire room all the way to the ceiling. I had no idea how bad it was.

I need to go through each bag and box to search for the bankbook. If it's not there, I'll add the box or bag to the mound in the kitchen. There's still room if I throw things to the back.

But the minute I find that money I'm going to pay Mum's debt, get her out of prison and then without even asking her, book a skip and fill it up. I'm not living with this junk any longer.

This gives me such a buzz, I work really hard, and after almost two hours, I've cleared a space all the way to what looks like a sofa. I feel like cheering, and then there's a thump on the front door.

I freeze.

"Josie? Let us in. It's me and Bazza."

Can they see me through the window? I think in terror. But the windows are covered. If I keep quiet they'll go away.

"Come on, girly, we know you're in there." Shirl's voice is hardening.

Then I hear a scratchy, scraping sound. When I peer into the hallway I see the front door open and crash against the chain. They've broken in! They're definitely real, live criminals if they can do that. Oh God!

"Deary me, was you scared of the police, Josie? That why you got the chain on?"

Shirl's voice sounds all gentle again and suddenly I feel unsure. Maybe they don't mean any harm. They just need somewhere to crash, and Mum did say that Shirl was really kind to her in prison.

"We brought you fish and chips to say thank you for letting us stay. How about it? We won't be in your hair more than another couple of days, eh, Bazza? Tell her?"

I hear Bazza cough a bit and then his dry, smoker's voice says, "I rung me bruvver, Tom. He lives by the sea with his wife and two kids. I need the fresh air for me lungs, and Tom says we can come on Tuesday, stay as long as we like."

"Why can't you go there now?" I call out.

"Ah, you're in there, thought you was!" Shirl gives a friendly laugh. "No, see, we can't go before Tuesday because he's got his old mum staying and there's no more room."

"She's ninety-two," says Bazza. "She stays with Tom one week and then me sister another week."

I have to admit it all sounds very different from what I had imagined. They're in between somewhere to stay because they've just come out of prison, and if Shirl was sharing with Mum, I don't think she can be a murderer. Maybe they just got into debt themselves. That doesn't make them dangerous. They're moving on in two days to stay with family and now I feel a bit mean being so suspicious.

"Okay," I call out, and I go down and take the chain off. I stare at them out on the pavement and then at the lock. "Have you broken it?"

"No." Shirl laughs out loud. "Bazza just messed about with a bit of wire because we thought maybe you'd locked yourself out."

"Okay, come in."

We all go up to Mum's room, and they lay out packets of fish and chips. Bazza's also bought twenty-four cans of beer and a six-pack of cola.

"What you been up to?" asks Shirl in her friendly-type voice.

"Homework," I say.

"Elaine said you studied all the time."

They chatter on together and manage to get through several cans each and half a pack of cigarettes. The room's too smoky for me. I make my excuses and go back to my own bedroom. I so wish Tash was here.

I closed up the living room before I opened the front door, so I don't think they know what I've done. But until they leave I can't go through the stuff. That means I've got to wait until Tuesday. What am I going to do until then?

My phone bleeps. It's a text. I grab it and press the button.

Training hard this week. What you up to? JP x

Only one kiss. Maybe he's just being polite. But at least he texted me. I don't know what to think. If Tasha was here, she'd know, wouldn't she? I have no one to ask.

And then I think of Mel. I could sneak out and go and see her. Maybe Len will be in a good mood too, and I can ask him more about paying Mum's debt. They might even help me go and visit Mum, or at least get a phone number so I can speak to her. Are prisoners allowed phone calls?

Feeling much more cheerful, I text back. *Just doing homework. Hope you got home okay. JT xx*

I sit staring at my screen for half an hour but he doesn't reply.

Nothing from Tasha either. Maybe she and her mum have

made up. They probably won't want me coming to stay. It looks like I'm stuck here with the prison gang all night.

The thought's so horrible I tiptoe to Mum's bedroom door. I can hear two different sets of snoring. With any luck they've drunk themselves into a stupor, so I skip downstairs and out of the house.

It's already dark, nearly six, and Mel will be cooking dinner for her grandparents. I'm really looking forward to seeing them again, especially Ivy. It's raining hard, so I jog along the streets with my hood up until I get to the door next to the pharmacy.

I ring on the doorbell, and after a couple of minutes I hear footsteps. Someone's standing behind the door. It must be Mel. Maybe she thinks social workers have come to take away Len, so I call through the mail slot, "It's me, Josie."

There's a rattling, and then Mel opens the door and hisses, "Come in, quick."

21.

Ivy greets me like an old friend.

"It's Josie—look, Len. Come and sit here, lovey. Plenty of room."

She pats the two-seater sofa and I sit down next to her. Len's glued to the telly in his usual chair. He doesn't look around, so I wonder if I'll be able to get anything out of him today.

Ivy's running on and on. "...And then Mel said we had to keep extra quiet because the nasty creep downstairs, that pet shop bloke—have you met him, lovey?"

I nod. "I think so; bald head?"

"That's the fella. Mr. Mooney, he calls himself—I'll give him mister!" She raises her tiny fist and shakes it around the room. "You know what he says to Mel yesterday? Tell her, Mel, stupid old creep."

Mel shakes her head and raises her eyebrows at me.

"He said," Ivy starts up again, "these flats ain't big enough for large families, and how long were we staying like. As if it's any of his business, I ask you." She leans forward and pokes Len on the arm. "Tell her what you said, Len."

Surprisingly Len turns around and opens his mouth. But nothing comes out so he just frowns and turns back to the television.

"Len said, tell him to call the council," says Ivy, and throws me a meaningful look. "But we don't want that, do we? Not if we're on the run from them."

Ivy falls silent, and Mel passes around plates of sandwiches.

It's so soothing to sit in a proper living room and have Sunday night tea around the television. This must be what normal families do. I decide that once I've got my flat—although I'll always have all my meals properly at the table, with matching plates and cutlery and paper napkins—on Sunday nights I'll have my tea just like Ivy and Len and Mel. Maybe I'll even invite them over.

"Have another sandwich, lovey. Plenty more, and then there's cream cakes."

Ivy's piling my plate and I grin through a mouthful of salmon and cucumber on crusty brown bread.

"How's the swimming going?" Mel's settled down in the other armchair.

"Not bad," I say. "I wanted to ask Len something about the council, but maybe..."

"He's not having a very good day," murmurs Mel. Then she says, "Why don't you help me with the washing up, Josie?"

We jump up and clear the plates. I'm dying to see Mel's kitchen, and of course, it's perfect. Matching cupboards and counters, a sparkling stainless-steel sink and drain board, everything neat and tidy. Surely me and Mum could have a kitchen just like this if we tidied up.

"Have you sorted things out with the council?" asks Mel as she fills a washing-up bowl and squirts in soap.

"Sort of," I say. "My mum sent me a letter to say my Grandpa Ted had left me some money, but I have to try and find the savings book. Then I can get the money and pay her debts."

"Can't be hard to find."

I give a snort. "You have no idea how much stuff my mum's collected."

As Mel washes and I dry with her newly laundered and ironed tea towel, I wonder if there might be enough money to pay the debt and then have a brand-new kitchen at home.

Once the kitchen's clean and tidy again, I go back into the living room, and Mel makes some fresh tea.

"Ooh!" squeals Ivy as I sit down. "I love this program. So does Len, don't you?" She pokes him again and he gives a grunt.

I look at the TV, and a woman's standing outside her house, saying, "I live a secret life, to tell the truth. No one ever comes inside."

The scene then changes to the front door, which is open a tiny crack. The commentator, a woman called Judy, is calling through the crack, "If you move a couple of boxes—yes, that's it—now I can get inside."

I feel this chill beginning to creep over me as I stare at the screen.

Judy's in the hallway now. The woman she's calling Nellie is saying, "If you climb over that pile, you can get down the hall to the stairs."

The camera shows Judy climbing and clambering through a hallway crammed to the ceiling with boxes and sacks and piles of newspapers.

"It must be very difficult living like this," says Judy.

"You get used to it," says Nellie. "But now I'd like to clear up. I want to invite my friends over for my sixtieth birthday. It's like living on a rubbish tip, if I'm honest."

A voiceover starts up as the camera continues through the

house. "There's a little hoarder in all of us. It's when it gets out of hand that it becomes a problem."

Every single room in the house is stuffed to the ceiling. There's no kitchen, almost no bathroom, no spare bedrooms, and Nellie's bedroom looks, well, just like Mum's. Half the bed's covered with sacks.

The voiceover continues, "Nellie's collection started thirty years ago, and it's been building up until it's completely swamped her. She's so attached to her hoard, she won't part with anything. Judy's going to help her try to make a start."

Judy's standing on the upstairs landing looking exhausted. "It's like a black wave coming toward me," she says.

Nellie just laughs and picks up a bag. "I've got more knickers than Marks and Sparks. This skirt's still got the price tag on."

"So you don't need any more," says Judy.

"Oh no, I'll buy more. I have to, you see."

The voiceover comes in again. "Nellie's an obsessive-compulsive hoarder. It will take a highly skilled therapist for her to understand why she hoards and how she can clear it and get her home back."

The program ends and the ads start up.

I sit there staring at the screen in shock.

That's *my* home! Exactly the same!

Nellie's just like my mum, and Judy's like Tasha, coming in and telling me that my mum's a hoarder. I feel so stupid I didn't listen, couldn't understand what Tasha was saying.

Everything makes sense now. All my life my mum has brainwashed me into believing we lived like that, completely differently from anyone else on the planet, because we were actually saving the planet.

But it's completely not true. There are hundreds of thousands of people all over the country who live like we do, and all of them keep it a total secret. They don't even know that there are other people living like them, in an obsessive-compulsive hoard.

The commentator said that Nellie had lost contact with her children because "they realized the hoard always came first, not them."

That's just like me. Mum doesn't buy me proper food, or school shoes, or anything. She just spends all her money on stupid things. Now she's in so much debt she's in prison, and it's all because of her stupid obsession with hoarding.

"Josie? Cake?" It's Mel. She's staring at me. She must have asked me a couple of times, but I was miles away.

I can't stay here. I feel so embarrassed and ashamed and naive. Ha, ha. That's what I called Tasha yesterday. She must be laughing and laughing at me. Everyone must be laughing at me. Ivy said this was her favorite program. Everyone must be watching it. It's popular, like all those documentaries about fat people. Everyone in school's always talking about the latest fat show and laughing at those poor people. Now I know—I'm absolutely certain—they know my mum's an obsessive hoarder just like all these people on telly, and they're talking about me behind my back.

Dom and Tasha will have told them about my house by now, won't they? All my secrets are out. I just want to run away and hide.

I stand up and mumble my thanks.

Ivy says in a hurt voice, "Why are you going? Are you upset, lovey? Is it something I said?"

Mel's clearing up the cups and she just nods at me. She's got her life almost sorted. She just needs to decide what to do with her grandparents. Why should she bother about me?

"No, Ivy, it's been lovely seeing you, really. I'll come again very soon."

As Ivy gives me a bright smile, her tiny bird eyes gleam away. I so wish I had a sweet little grandma to worry over me. There's only Mum, and after seeing that program, I think I totally hate her now.

My mum's been lying to me all my life, I think, as I stride home, hands in my pockets, shaking with fury. She's ruined my life. Why should I bother to try to get her out of prison? She can rot there forever for all I care. I haven't even asked Mel how I could phone the prison. Right now I never want to speak to Mum again!

I let myself in and slam the door behind me. The boxes in the hall shiver and seem to loom toward me. I can hear Shirl and Bazza talking and laughing away and the living room door is open.

The anger surging through me hits the top note. Pushing my way down the hall, I go into the living room and yell, "What the hell are you doing in here? Get out! In fact, get the hell out of my house, right now!"

They turn and stare at me, Bazza with a cigarette drooping from his thin lips. They look like such a couple of tramps. Why did I let them back in? Shirl doesn't even try to put on her cold smile. Instead she nods at Bazza. He continues to stare at me but his hand reaches into the top of his boot and he pulls out the biggest knife I've ever seen. It has a wide blade that ends in a horrid cruel point. My blood turns to ice.

Slowly he hefts the knife in his hand and then begins to clean his filthy nails with the point.

"This is how it's going to be," says Shirl, and her voice is pure poison, no mock-friendly tone now. "We're going to stick around for a bit, find that bankbook, and then you'll get the money out for us. We're a bit short at the moment, girly—you know how it is. So why don't you help us? Go and sort out the kitchen, because the sooner we get our money, the sooner we'll be gone. Right, Bazza?"

Bazza takes the blade out of his nail and points it lazily at me and then around the room. "Right, Shirl."

"No," I say, and although my voice is wobbling, I've stuck my chin in the air. I'm sick of being pushed around by everyone and brainwashed. No one is real, no one is the person they pretend to be, including my mum and Tasha and Dom and even Jordan. If he liked me, why doesn't he want to see me? He's not a real person if he's going to judge me by my mum's house. This isn't my fault.

"*This* is how it's going to be," I say, and Shirl and Bazza exchange grins, which only makes me more angry.

"I'm going to the police now, and they're going to come and arrest you."

They don't move. They don't even look worried.

I start back toward the front door. I can wriggle out of my house twice as quick as them and be down the street at a run before they get to the front door.

"You do that," calls Shirl. "Then you'll be in a foster home before midnight and you'll never get your mum out."

I stop in my tracks. Oh God, she's right. I'm sixteen on Thursday, but that's another five days, and anyway you have to be eighteen before they let you live by yourself. That's what Tasha says.

I stop and turn. "Okay, you win," I say in a weary voice. "But get on with it and get out."

They don't say anything, which is a relief. Bazza kicks a couple of boxes and Shirl starts tearing open a plastic bag. My heart sinks when I think of them stealing our, no, my money. Grandpa Ted left it to *me*.

Then I hear a tapping on the front door. I glance in the living room but the tramps don't seem to have heard. I squeeze down to the door and open it. Tasha's on the street and she's sobbing silently and shaking.

I grab her and hiss, "Don't make a sound. Follow me."

She nods and we go inside and close the front door with only a tiny click. Then we creep past the living room and upstairs to my room. Once inside, I turn the key in the lock.

"They're back," says Tasha. "What happened? And don't think that will keep them out. Chaz got through everything I jammed against my door."

"I've been so stupid, Tasha, so unbelievably stupid." Then I tell her how Shirl and Bazza wheedled their way back in and how they've threatened me now. I also tell her about the hoarder program. "So now I know what you meant. You're probably all laughing at me, and everyone in school is too."

"Who's laughing? Me and Dom? Don't be mad. We haven't told anyone. You're not stupid, Josie Tate. You're really clever; I know because my sweet little Dom is a brainbox, and you're a bit like him."

Tasha has stopped crying and wiped her eyes. She's got a backpack over her shoulder, and she empties it onto the bed. "See, that's all my worldly goods now. A few pairs of pants, T-shirts and shorts, couple of pairs of tights and my school uniform."

"Your mum didn't listen, then."

She gives a snort. "'Chaz is the best thing that ever happened to me,'" she says in a voice that mimicks her mum.

“ ‘Chaz is a good man, and he’d never do anything to harm you. Chaz says he’s tried to be like a father to you. Chaz says you’re making all this up because you’re jealous. Chaz says . . .’ ” She stops as though something has stuck in her throat.

Then she picks up Mickey Mouse, and, cuddling him tight against her chest, she says, “What am I going to do now, Josie? I’m so scared of ending up in a cardboard box on the streets.”

22. Tasha

I'm homeless now.

Or I've left home. Almost definitely.

But at least I'm not sleeping in a doorway.

Mum said yesterday, "I don't think you can stay here right now, Tasha. Go back to Dom's, and let me know when you've come to your senses."

But I'm not staying at Dom's. I'm sharing a bed with Josie Tate, whose mum's in prison and who lives in a hoarder house taken over by two ex-cons with a big knife and a smoking habit.

So I'm not totally homeless because I have actually got a roof over my head, but I might be pretty soon because it's really dangerous in Josie's house right now.

Mum has chosen Chaz instead of me, and my school uniform's beginning to reek.

I asked Josie about washing clothes last night.

"I go to the launderette once a week," she said.

Mum's given me twenty quid. She said I should text her when I need more, and she'll drop it off at school in an envelope for me. Like, thanks.

So I've skipped afternoon school and I'm in the launderette in no underwear, a horrid brown skirt and T-shirt I found in the hoard. Josie and I use that word now; finally, she's seen the light. Everything I own is going around and around in the washing machine.

Tasha's Vlog

Monday, October 21, 2:46 p.m.

I'm vlogging in the launderette. There's wifi coming through the wall from the upstairs flat, I think, but the signal's a bit weak. Josie and I have become best mates. I'm so glad I didn't spread it all around school about her mum being a hoarder. In the old days meano Tasha Brown would have done just that. But since Josie let me stay, even before she knew about Chaz, it just didn't seem right to betray her. And now we're a team because we have to try to survive in the house with the criminals.

Signal disappears.

A lady with a dog on a leash comes in. Not that I care if anyone hears me anymore. I've got enough problems to worry about.

She empties one of the dryers, taking ages to fold all her clothes. I keep stabbing the laptop to see if the signal has come back.

Just as the lady leaves, the signal returns.

Record.

Takes ages for the clothes to wash in here. Not that I've got anywhere else to go. I'm not going back to the house until Josie's home.

We lay awake half the night whispering

about how we can get rid of Shirl and Bazza. Josie says she doesn't care about the money anymore, but she's mad as hell at those two for pulling a knife on her. Maybe I can get hold of a gun, she said at one point. I bet Mum's got one somewhere in her hoard. Why not? She's got everything else.

You're mad, I said. A gun tops a knife, said Josie, and her green eyes were gleaming in the light from her clock radio. I'm not going to let them win, she said, and I believe her, I really do, but I'm so scared. I didn't let Mickey go all night.

But mostly I lay there thinking about Mum and how she won't listen to me. Does that mean she doesn't love me anymore? Or maybe she never loved me. Josie says her mum loves her, she knows she does, but she doesn't *care* enough about her, like with food and clothes and a clean house and stuff. I always thought I came from a good home because I always had everything I wanted. Mum even sent me on the school ski trip last year. I don't have to get a job for the things I need, like food. Josie has to buy most of her own food and she eats rubbish. I can't afford fruit, she said to me last week when I dared to ask for an apple.

Signal fades.

This is driving me mental. Our wifi at home never fails. The washing's finished, and I shove it all in the dryer. I've never done my own washing before. Mum does all that, and she keeps the flat clean and tidy. I never thought before about my home, but now after staying with Josie and then those awful crowded nights with Dom, I can see what a nice home Mum made for us.

But she doesn't love me.

Dom's mum would do anything for him, and Josie's mum loves her, at least. Even though, as Josie said last night, love's not enough.

"You can't brainwash someone, even if you do love them."

Her voice was getting so loud I had to hush her back down again.

Then she said, "If you love someone, you make sure they're safe and have everything they need, like food and hot water for showers and clean clothes. Instead, my mum ends up in prison, leaves me in our disgusting home and sends those criminals around to rip us off."

"We've both been ripped off by our mums," I said. Then I felt so miserable I started to cry again.

"You can stay here for as long as you like," Josie said.

"Your mum won't want me here when she gets home."

"She doesn't decide anymore. I'm so sick of her and all her lies. . . ."

"Both our mums lie."

We were silent for ages after that, and then we heard Shirl and Bazza talking in the hallway. Their speech was slurred as if they were drunk again. I couldn't make out everything they said, but then Shirl said in a really loud voice, "And if those little madams think they can tell us what to do, well, you'll be ready, Bazza, won't you?"

"Yes, Shirl—keeping me blade nice and sharp."

I heard Josie moan under the duvet. I had my end stuffed in my mouth so I wouldn't scream out. I have never been so terrified in all my life, not even when Chaz was coming on to me. Maybe it would be safer sleeping in a doorway in the streets.

We lay under the duvet for hours. I was sobbing silently all over poor Mickey again. Finally the house went totally silent, and I dared to whisper, "You awake?"

"I'm planning how to get that gun. I'm going to blast their brains into next year."

"I'll polish the bullets," I said, and we both shook with silent giggles. "And Dom can do the math so we line up the barrel correctly."

"What about Jordan?" whispered Josie.

"He can mop up the blood."

We shook again under the cover, and then Josie sat up and put on her bedside light. "Hungry?"

"I could eat an elephant," I said.

"Well, I haven't got an elephant, but this might do."

She reached over the bed, pulled up a heavy-looking carrier bag and tipped it onto the duvet.

"Wow! It's a feast!" I said.

The bed was covered with packs of crisps, huge bars of chocolate, blocks of cheese, packets of crackers and a huge bag of apples.

"A midnight feast," said Josie, grinning. "And you have to eat *all* the apples. Too healthy for me!"

> *Record.*
> This is probably my last chance to do the vlog before my clothes dry and the signal goes for good. But what I really want to say is that

homeless people can get food and get their clothes clean. If they know someone like Josie Tate, they can even find a bed for the night.

But how do you make your mum love you and put you before her pervy boyfriend? Josie thinks that Chaz will slip up very soon, and Mum will see what he's really like. But I'm not so sure.

I thought I knew my mum, but now I'm beginning to think about all the times she didn't cuddle me when I fell down or help me with my homework or expected me to play by myself in my room for hours and hours while she went on Internet dating sites.

My mum can make the right sort of home.

But what use is a nice home if you're not loved and wanted?

23. Josie

In the cold light of day, I realize I can never get hold of a gun. Even if I did, would I honestly have the guts to shoot Shirl and Bazza? The thought makes me laugh as Tasha and I go out of the house at seven. It's a freezing morning, and the hole in my shoe is swirling cold air around my toes.

"Go and wait for me in Terry's Café, and we'll have breakfast before school," I tell Tasha.

She huddles down in her jacket and walks off. She looks so small. Is she getting thinner? She doesn't eat as much as me, and food is very hit-and-miss at the moment. Another problem to solve: How do I keep Tasha alive while I get rid of the tramps?

As I plod through my paper route, I wonder how long it will take them to find the pink makeup bag with Grandpa's bankbook. Even if they do find it, I have no idea how we would take the money out. The bank won't exactly hand over thousands to a kid like me or two losers like them. That's my only hope really, that they realize they can't get the money and they disappear before someone calls the police.

I've almost given up the idea of paying the debt and getting Mum out. Why hasn't she rung me again? Even cold-blooded killers are allowed to ring home.

I meet Tasha, and after breakfast we go off to school.

She texts me at lunchtime. *Going to launderette now. Meet me to go home together? xx T*

I text back. *Sure. Terrys 4.*

I'm in the library and I've Googled Fenton Prison, but their website doesn't tell you how you can call a prisoner. I'm too scared to ring Enquiries by myself. Everyone keeps looking over my shoulder and trying to see what I'm looking up. There's no privacy in this place.

I can't be bothered to do any work. I start thinking about how me and Tasha were joking around last night, talking about guns and bullets. Tasha said Jordan's job would be to mop up the blood. I smile again when I think of immaculate Jordan down on his hands and knees on our filthy, blood-soaked carpet.

But now a picture of the first time we met flashes into my mind. I was the one scrabbling about on the floor, and when I first saw him, I thought he was naked. I got that wrong and was so embarrassed but I still couldn't help noticing his gorgeous, toned, muscular, golden body.

You don't need makeup, Josie. You have such beautiful green eyes, like the sea. I like you just normal.

His words from our date on Saturday night whisper in my ear again. When we danced close in the gig, his lips brushed my cheek and it felt like silk.

Jordan!

Why did I let him go? I must be mad!

It's like I've been struck by lightning.

I leap up, stuff my books into my pack, ignore the bell for

final lesson of the day and stride out of school. I don't even wait for the bus but break into a jog and run all the way to the launderette just as Tasha's coming out.

"Stop, Tash! Wait up." I'm out of breath. All I can do is stand in front of her, my lungs heaving for air.

"Where's the fire, babes?" she says.

Finally I get my breath back and say, "I have to go out tonight."

Her eyes widen in terror. "You can't leave me on my own with them, Josie, please."

"I have to go and see Jordan," I say. "Why should I let my mum ruin everything? Jordan's the first boy ever to notice me. I have to go to his house and try again. I can't give up. . . ."

Tasha shakes her head sadly. "I thought that's what I could do with Rory, but I'm not getting anywhere."

"He's never asked you out. Get real, Tash. It's different with me and Jordan."

Her face shuts down and I feel so mean. I say, "Look, let's go back to the house, I have to change. His parents live in this gated palace—"

"Gated!"

"They're rich. I can't go looking like this. Will you help me?"

"If you promise not to leave me home with *them.*"

"Promise," I say.

When we get to the house and go inside, we can hear the tramps rummaging around in the living room again.

As we walk past I sneer, "Found anything yet?"

"No," says Shirl, but her face doesn't look so sure anymore. "But we will."

I give a snort. "How do you know there's anything there? My mum has a serious mental condition."

I hear Tasha gasp behind me. I stiffen, but I don't care anymore. What have I got to lose?

"My mum's called an obsessive-compulsive hoarder. She needs a psychiatrist, not a prison. My grandpa died fourteen years ago. I bet Mum's spent that money, and she's forgotten all about it."

"No, she ain't," says Shirl. "I was in the cell with her; she told me the whole situation. She couldn't have spent it. There's only rubbish here."

"Yeah, right," I say, with an even bigger sneer on my face. "Look around you. This house is stuffed to the roof, and all of it"—I wave my hand about—"was bought and paid for in secondhand shops. So where do you think she got the cash, eh?"

Then I grab Tasha's arm and we push off up the stairs and into my room, laughing into our hands.

"You're a total legend, Josie Tate!" splutters Tasha, and I feel about ten feet tall.

I'm so fired up now, I'm ready to take on the world. If that means getting through the gate into Jordan's house and demanding that he tells me to my face that he dumped me, then bring it on.

I change my clothes. Tasha does my makeup and hair. We agree that she'll come with me and wait at the bus stop.

We go out of the house and slam the door as hard as we can, rattling the windows. Bazza comes out a few seconds later and yells at us, but Tasha just makes a rude gesture and we go off arm in arm, giggling as loud as we can.

When we finally part at the top of Jordan's road, I suddenly feel all my courage disappear and my knees go weak and wobbly. What if he won't see me? Or his parents won't let me in?

I arrive at the gate and my finger hovers over the buzzer. Just do it, Josie Tate, I tell myself. What have you got to lose? Everything, I think, and then I press the buzzer.

Silence.

I stand there wondering if I should press again, and then I hear a sound and the gate clicks. I push it open and I'm in.

This time when I walk up the drive to the front door, it's shut tight; no one's waiting to greet me. Just as I think I'm going to have to bang on the door—I can't see a bell anywhere—it opens and Jordan comes out. He closes the door behind him.

"Hi," he says.

His hands are shoved into the pockets of his jeans and he's wearing a Torpedoes sweatshirt, with the hood up as if for protection. His almond eyes are sunk into their sockets, eyebrows creased in a worried frown.

"You want to talk out here?" I say in a cold voice, only I wobble on the last word.

He nods. "Let's walk around the garden."

I follow him down the side of the house and what looks like a farm spreads out before us. A huge expanse of manicured lawn stretches down a gentle slope to a small wood. Beyond, the countryside opens out. It's a clear evening and the hills in the distance spread like a soft blue line along the horizon.

"Wow!" I say, even though I'm trying to be cold and distant.

"Yeah, it's a nice view. We can walk down to the woods if you like."

"Sure."

He takes my hand in a light grip, and I don't pull away. We walk over the grass and into the woods.

"Here," he says.

There's a seat carved out of a fallen tree, but it looks quite damp. I hesitate, and he fishes a plastic bag out of his pocket and lays it down carefully.

I sit down.

He takes my hand again and I say, "What've you been up to?"

"Just training, nothing special."

"Oh."

Then he turns to me and there's such a look of anguish on his face. I think there are tears welling in his eyes.

This is it, I tell myself, stiffening inside. He's fallen for Chantelle, and who can blame him? She's gorgeous and rich like him, and I bet she doesn't have a mother in pr—

"I'm so sorry, Josie!" He bursts through all my thoughts. "I've done something so dumb, but I don't care. I'm not going to let it change things. I'm not going to let them . . ." His voice breaks down, and he can't catch his breath.

"Whoa! Steady on," I say.

He's thrown himself to his feet and drops my hand. I think he's going to walk off and leave me here, and I won't find my way out through the gate. Panic rises in me. Then I see him grappling in the pocket of his jeans and he pulls out something gray. It's a puffer.

Jordan has asthma? How does he swim like that?

He pumps twice and breathes in deeply and his shoulders drop as he begins to relax. He puts the puffer away and turns around to me. "Sorry," he says. He doesn't sit down.

"Don't be stupid," I snap, still feeling quite spooked. "It's not your fault. I didn't know, that's all."

He's still standing, and now he turns and looks down the wood, his hands stuffed in his pockets, shoulders hunched.

"I didn't think you could swim with asthma, that takes real guts," I say.

"You're the brave one, Josie," he says and gives a snorty kind of laugh. "I'm a stinking coward. You have no idea."

"It's okay," I say, "I get it; you want to finish with me after Saturday night."

I stand up and pick up the plastic bag and start to fold it. We're done here, I think. It was fun while it lasted.

But Jordan swings around and places his hands on my shoulders so firmly that I'm rooted to the spot.

"Okay, yeah," he says. "I was upset when I found out your mom's in prison, and I didn't really get your house. But the worst thing I did, the absolute worst thing, was I came home and told Mom and Dad. Not about your house," he finishes, his voice trailing off.

"Okay," I say. So why does he say he's a coward?

"No, it's not okay, Josie. I'll spell it out for you, and then you can dump me, like I know you'll want to. I told Mom and Dad that your mom's in prison, and they didn't even ask why. They just said that this would ruin my swim career; I'd never get onto the Olympic team if it all comes out."

"Okay," I say again. What would most parents say?

"No, don't you see. They said I could *never* see you again."

His eyes are wider than I've ever seen them, and they're on fire, blazing away at me. In that moment all I want to do is kiss him. But I can't. We're finished, aren't we?

"I can see that your mum and dad wouldn't want you going

out with a convict's daughter," I say. "And let's face it: most parents would feel the same."

"Yes! Yes, of course they would!"

"So, I'll go." I try to wriggle free but his hands have me pinned down, and Jordan's so strong and muscular I can't move. I feel close to tears.

"Don't you see?" he says again in a louder voice. "That's why I'm such a stinking, worthless coward! I agreed! I said I would never see you again so that I can go on swimming and competing and winning medals and make it to the Olympics."

"Sure," I say. "I totally get it."

Jordan's not even listening. His skin looks as though it's stretched tight across his cheekbones and he opens his mouth and yells, "But I DON'T AGREE!"

He's shouting now and the woods have a tiny echo, like Rory's chant at the gig, and the sound comes back to us faintly through the trees: *don't agree.*

We both stand there in silence and then Jordan yells again, "I DON'T AGREE!"

And the echo throws it back: *don't agree.*

I give myself a little shake and then I stare hard at Jordan and say, "What?"

"I don't care what my parents say. It's not your fault your mom's in prison, and it's not your fault how you live. It's up to your mom to get her life together. You're the best friend, and first and therefore *best* girlfriend I ever had. It can all go hang—my swim career, Mom and Dad. . . . If I'm not allowed to choose my friends and my girlfriends—girlfriend—then it's all worthless."

His head slumps down and I reach up, pull his hood back and stroke the top of his head. We stand like that for ages.

Then Jordan looks up at me and whispers, “We okay?”

“Sure,” I whisper back.

He puts his forehead against mine, and we lean into each other.

Then he kisses me for so long, I lose all sense of time and place.

24. Tasha

I wait for hours and hours at the bus stop, and then I see Josie walking toward me. I can tell straight away that she's all loved up. A pang of loneliness goes through me. Will Rory ever return my love?

"So it went okay?" I ask.

"Mmm."

"And his mum and dad?"

"He doesn't care."

The bus comes and we sit down, and then as it pulls away she talks nonstop about how Jordan's parents wanted him to dump her because her mum's in prison and how he stood up to them. "…And then he said I'm his girlfriend, and he, you know," she blushes and looks down.

"Loves you," I finish and give her a hug. "Brilliant."

"Jordan says it's not my fault Mum's a hoarder or she's in prison. He loves me, and his parents can put up or shut up."

"He actually said that? Didn't know he had it in him."

"Tasha!"

"What?"

We burst into howling laughter and don't stop until we get off the bus.

We're still giggling and talking in loud voices when we go in the house. Then Bazza is right in front of us in the hall, blocking the way.

I feel myself shrivel inside, but Josie sticks her chin in the air and says, "Excuse us, we're going upstairs."

"Not so fast," says Bazza, and the knife appears from behind his back.

I stuff my fist in my mouth to stop myself from screaming out loud.

"What do you want?" says Josie, and her voice has a real edge to it. She must be scared but she's not going to show him.

"We've gone through that room and we ain't found nothing. Shirl's gone up the prison to see your mum, and she'd better come back with the right answer. If we don't find that money..."

He hefts the knife from one hand to the next.

"We'll all go to the police," says Josie.

"They'll take you into care," he says with a nasty grin. "I been in care. It's worse than prison."

Josie tosses her head. Honestly, I think she's the bravest person I've ever met.

"Nothing could be worse than being here with you two," she says.

She grabs my arm and walks toward Bazza, and amazingly he sidesteps into the living room and lets us pass.

Once we're in the bedroom and the door's locked, I grab Josie and say, "You are incredible! Weren't you scared?"

"Yes, but if they were going to kill us they'd have done it by now. They know that our friends have seen them, so there are witnesses. We just have to sitick it out, Tash, and hope that Mum tells them where the money is."

Josie's managed to smuggle the kettle full of water into our room, so we make black coffee and finish up the food from last night. We settle down in bed with Josie's radio playing quietly until we drift off to sleep.

Then her alarm is going off and the radio's telling us it's six thirty. Josie creeps out of bed, unlocks the door and goes out. When she comes back, she whispers, "They're spark out as usual, hungover with any luck."

We pull on our uniforms, grab our stuff and leave the house. I wait for Josie in Terry's while she does her paper route. We have breakfast and then shower in the phys ed block at school.

What a life, I think, as I shampoo my hair. No proper facilities, nowhere to cook and two criminals threatening us with knives. At least when I lived at home with Mum, I was safe and fed. I never knew that people lived such difficult lives. Even without the criminals, Josie's had it really tough, but I never heard her moan at school. She's amazing—she can cope with anything.

At the bottom of everything I can see that she really loves her mum. Whenever I saw them together, you could tell they cared about each other. Well, her mum better make some real changes in her life. Josie's getting so brave, I wouldn't blame her if she left home forever.

Like me, I think. Only my mum couldn't care less.

As we take the bus to school, I say to Josie, "Do you think your mum told them where the money is?"

"I don't think she knows, and anyway, they're still here."

"If we go to the police, you'll go into care, and I'll have to live with Mum and Chaz. That can't happen, Josie. Not ever."

She's very quiet. She doesn't have a real plan, does she?

Which means I have to come up with a way to get rid of those two.

We go in opposite directions once we get to school, but I can't face class. All I want to do is talk to my vlog. Maybe by talking out loud I can come up with a plan, so I sneak into an empty classroom and log on.

> Tasha's Vlog
> Tuesday, Oct 22, 9:05 a.m.
> It's nice and quiet in here. Wish I could hang out all day, maybe even sleep here. Who would notice? I bet I could find a sleeping bag in the hoard. There's a rickety old cupboard at the back of the classroom where I could keep it.
>
> *Camera pans room.*
>
> Here's the cupboard, and here's the blinds to close when I go to sleep. There's the plug for my laptop and phone. What else does a girl want? But—*big sigh, tragic face*—I don't have time for all this. I need to come up with a plan to get rid of the criminals.
>
> *Pause.*

Trouble is, I can't think of anything. We can't call the police, we're not strong enough to push them out the door and we can't give them what they want.

Oh!

> *Record.*
> Bingo! I know exactly what they want, don't I? *Toothy grin like Mickey.* They want Josie's money, so the best thing I can do is help them find it, and then they'll disappear.

Clicks fingers at the screen. Just like that!

I slam my laptop shut, shove it in my bag and walk out of school before anyone notices me. I'm back at the hoarder house before nine thirty, hammering on the door.

Eventually Shirl opens up. "Yeah?" she growls, her eyes still blurry from sleep.

"I've come to help look for the money," I say.

"Finally come to your senses. Where's your mate?"

"Er, well, she has an exam this morning."

She looks me up and down, and then she lets me in. "You start on the little room upstairs at the back of the house," she says. "We're doing the kitchen."

"Okay," I say, but as I slither between her podgy body and the piled boxes, she grabs me by the shoulder and puts her face close to mine. "If you find the money, you give it to us, right!"

Her voice grates like razor blades, and I nod furiously, my teeth chattering from fear.

Shirl gives me a shove and I feel her eyes boring into my back as I go upstairs.

I haven't even noticed that there's another door at the end of the upstairs landing. There's no light and no windows. But then I see it, and when I push the door it only gives a few centimeters. The room must be stuffed to the ceiling like the rest of the house. I reach my hand through the gap. My arm's so thin, I can get most of it inside.

My hand closes around a plastic sack. I manage to pull it through the gap, and then pull out a couple more bags. Eventually the door opens wide enough for me to get inside. I was right: the windows, walls...everything is covered with the hoard. I've never seen anything like it.

Come on, Tasha Brown, I tell myself. Open every single thing and find that bankbook. Then those two will leave, and Josie and I can sleep safe at night. At least until her mum comes home, which is still a few weeks away if the debt isn't paid.

I open half the boxes and bags in the room and wade through mounds of clothes, papers, books, tins of food, plastic bottles and loads of pathetic ornaments.

But no sign of that stupid bankbook.

After three hours I'm shattered. I sneak to the top of the stairs. I can't hear anything, so I quickly change out of my uniform into a long-sleeved T-shirt and jeans, grab my jacket and bag and tiptoe downstairs.

There's a murmur coming from the kitchen. Bazza and Shirl are crouched on the floor rifling through boxes of what looks like booze, laughing and murmuring together. They're so absorbed they don't look around.

I turn into the hallway and squeeze my way toward the front door. My heart leaps as I reach the knob and I'm about to turn it when Bazza yells, "Stop right there, you little bitch!"

I freeze, my heart thumping like Rory's drummer. My legs won't work. I have to open the door and run out but I can't. I'm not brave like Josie.

"Have you found that money?" snarls Shirl. "You little cow, I bet you're trying to run away with it."

"No, I'm not," I say in a weak voice.

"Come back here so we can search you," says Bazza. "She's a little liar, ain't she, Shirl!"

"She's asking for a smack in the mouth!"

The thought of Shirl slapping my face is so horrendous that my body jerks into action. I turn, grab the door and wrench it open but at the same moment, Bazza yells, "Little bitch!" and something slams into the back of my head. It falls down my back, bruising me all the way, and lands on the floor. It's a tin of beans.

For a second I think I'm going to black out, but I manage to shove myself through the doorway and stagger out into the street. There are people walking along the pavement both ways. I glance behind me and see Bazza and Shirl peer out the door. I'm already halfway down the street, looking over my shoulder every second. But they don't seem to want to risk following me and trying to drag me back in front of all these people. I'd scream blue murder.

I'm free, and I've got to stay free. The bus stop's up ahead, and a bus is pulling up. I've got to run, ignore my woozy head and the feeling of wet stickiness falling down the back of my neck. I'm sure I'm bleeding, but there's no time to worry about that now.

I force my legs forward, and just as the driver turns on his blinker to pull out, I reach the doors and bang on them. He stares at me, and then reluctantly opens up again and I'm in. I swipe my bus pass, stagger to a seat and slump down.

It's midday on Tuesday morning and I have nowhere to go. I put my hand up to the back of my head and it comes away covered in bright red blood.

"You need to get that checked out, dear."

I turn my head. An Indian lady in a beautiful green head scarf, as green as Josie's eyes, is staring at me with a concerned look.

For a minute everything goes blurry, and I think it's Josie come to get me.

Then the lady speaks again. "The bus goes past the hospital. I can take you into accident and emergency if you like."

"I can take myself," I say, turning back. I can't risk anyone asking lots of questions. If I go by myself I can make up a story.

"Next stop, then," says the lady. "Go carefully, and Allah be with you."

I hope He is, because right now I need everyone's god to keep me safe.

I get off the bus and cross the street to the emergency department. It's not very busy, and within ten minutes a doctor's examining me.

"We'll stitch you up, Tasha. Then we need to keep you in overnight," says the doctor.

"What! Why? I need to, er, get back to school."

"You seem quite woozy, and you might have a concussion. We can't let you go home with a head wound like that. We need to telephone your mum. Can you give the nurse the number please?"

I close my eyes and lean back and I hear them murmuring. Then I feel a sharp prick in the back of my head as the doctor starts to work away on the wound. He's put me on my side, and I lie there with my eyes closed.

But I'm thinking away, making my next plan.

"There, all done. The nurse will come back in a few minutes and take your details."

"Mm, okay," I murmur, keeping my eyes closed.

Everything falls silent around me. I cautiously open my eyes. I'm alone. The wound's aching like mad, and there's a large bandage over my head. When I put my legs down on the floor I feel dizzy, but I steady myself and my head clears a bit.

Time to disappear, I tell myself, and I peer around the

curtain. No one's there, so I grab my jacket and bag from the chair and slip away, out of the hospital and back to the bus stop before anyone spots me.

Now what, Tasha Brown? I ask myself. I stand shaking and shivering as it begins to rain. Cardboard box in a doorway tonight?

25. Tasha

Tasha's Vlog

Tuesday October 22, 3:47 p.m.

Everyone will be coming out of school soon. I so want to see Dom, but this bandage looks crazy weird. I'm back in the launderette, and I've just been dozing for the last hour. It's quiet and warm in here with the dryers on. I like watching the clothes go around and around, getting all nice and clean. Josie said last night that her dream is to get her own flat and keep it spotless all the time. "I won't have anything in it," she said. "Well, only the things I absolutely need."

I so understand. Her home's filthy—nowhere to wash—and I'd never do a number two on a toilet with the door open. I spend half my day deciding where to go to the loo. I so hate showering in school. The showers are full of everyone's manky hairs and squashed shampoo bottles. I thought Josie

would be used to it, but she says you never get
used to it.

Pause.

My phone bleeps. It's a text from Dom.

in terrys exams all done come over? xx dom

My eyes well up. I'm so desperate to see him, but I can't go looking like this. I feel up the side of my head and start to unravel the bandage. It makes me feel a bit woozy again, but I keep on winding and winding until it's all off. I think about throwing it away, but then I stop. Maybe it will come in useful. I can wash it next time I bring my laundry down here. I fold it up carefully and put it in my backpack. Somehow that makes me feel so scared and lonely and even more like a homeless person than ever. All I have in the world is in this bag.

I have nowhere to sleep tonight, and neither does Josie.

I text Dom back. *be there in ten xx tash xx*

Record.

I look better without the bandage, and my hair is almost covering the dressing over the wound. I'll tell Dom I fell over in P.E. He knows how unphysical I am. Maybe he'll let me stay over tonight. But what about Josie?

I pack away my laptop, but I feel so tired I lie down on the bench with my head on my pack and close my eyes. Just a couple of minutes rest, I tell myself.

When I open my eyes again, it's pitch-dark outside and a dog's licking my face.

"Come on," says a rough voice.

A man's standing over me. He has a tattoo on his neck and a shaved head. There's a huge bunch of keys clinking in his hand.

"Off you go. This ain't no homeless hostel."

I pull myself up, swing my pack onto my shoulder and go outside. My phone says ten past five, and there are ten missed calls and texts from Dom.

It's only a short walk to Terry's, but it's blowing a gale, and the rain's gushing down. I zip my jacket up, but I'm soaked in seconds. By the time I push through the café door, I feel like a drowned rat.

Dom's sitting at a table with Jordan and Josie, and Freckly Emily's leaning on Dom's shoulder. They're looking at some papers and laughing. Jordan has his arm around Josie's shoulders, and she's leaning her head on his cheek. They all look so happy and, well, loved up.

Then Freckly says, "That's brilliant, Dom. I knew you'd solve it. Move the *x*. Genius."

She leans over and gives him a kiss on the cheek. A stab of pain goes right through me as I watch Dom smile back.

Freckly catches sight of me and says to Dom, "Have to go. See you at math club on Friday?" She pats his arm and he nods and mumbles his good-byes.

I should be so happy for him, I tell myself—his first proper girlfriend. Freckly is clever like him, so she knows what to talk about.

But a part of me is breaking in two. If I don't have my sweet little Dom anymore, then who's on my side against the dark and the rain?

"Where've you been, Tish Tash? I've been calling and calling." Dom grabs my arm and pulls me over.

Jordan and Josie go off to get more coffees and I say, "She's nice."

"Emily? She's got an amazing brain."

He seems so casual, but then maybe he's sparing my feelings. I've told him so often that I'm mad in love with Rory—Am I still?—so maybe he doesn't want to admit he's fallen for Brainbox Emily until Rory asks me out. Which feels like never. My feelings are washing around inside me at full spin. I feel quite dizzy.

The others come back with the coffees and Josie says, "We need to get home soon."

"Do we?" says Jordan.

"You know what we agreed," says Josie in a teasing tone. "You don't want to upset your parents anymore. . . . Hey, Tash, what's up?"

I seem to have dropped my coffee and it's dripping all over my clothes. More washing, I think, as my head droops and Dom lets out a low whistle.

"Tish Tash, what's happened?" His fingers are reaching up to my head.

I can hear myself muttering just like an old tramp, wandering along the streets, all alone. No one will listen, no one cares. "So I went back to the house and said I'd help to find the money. . . ."

"Why? God, Tasha! All by yourself with those pigs!" Josie's voice almost breaks. She's so angry with me. I don't blame her.

"Had to do something," I mutter. "Had to get the house back for us, get rid of the crims. I've got nowhere else to sleep, and now I'm on the streets. Can't go back there."

"Are you crazy?" That's Jordan and he sounds quite scared. "Josie, you're not sleeping on the streets. What's going on in your house?"

I hear Josie filling them in about Shirl and Bazza. "But I can handle them," she finishes in her brave voice.

"Not anymore," I say. "They threw a can of beans at my head today. I've got ten stitches. Bazza wants to kill us."

Dom grabs me. He holds me so tight I almost stop breathing. He's so warm and safe and kind. I never want him to let me go. Why aren't we brother and sister living together with his lovely mum and dad and even all his smelly little brothers? I wouldn't care how crowded and poor we were. If only someone loved me. Only me.

Then Dom's speaking and he's saying, "Why didn't you tell me, Tasha? I told you, I can fix anything. You don't need to do this all by yourself. I'm always here for you."

His voice sinks into me like a warm blanket, wrapping around my heart and lungs and stomach, filling me with hope.

"*And* you'll never be on the streets because you're going to live with me and my mum," says Josie. "Okay, Dom, what's the plan?"

Dom has released one arm but he keeps holding me tight with the other. I can feel him punching numbers on his phone. "Jordan, mate, I need to make a few phone calls. Can you take Tasha?"

"Sure," says Jordan, and then he's wrapped an arm around one side of me and Josie the other. I'm sandwiched between the two like a delicate glass ornament that everyone thinks will break if they let it go. For the first time in ages, I actually feel safe.

I open my eyes and watch Dom walk across the café, speaking into his phone. "Angel, yeah.... No.... Sasha and Pasha."

It's almost as though he's grown a little as he takes charge. Josie keeps saying he's, well, into me. Is he? More to the point, am I into him?

I hear him give Josie's address, and then he comes back with a huge grin on his face. "Sorted," he said.

"What can Angel do?" I say as the other two drift back together.

Dom puts his arm around me again. I can't help noticing how we fit together like two pieces of a jigsaw.

"You haven't met Angel's boyfriend, Sasha," says Dom, but I'm hardly listening as I breathe in his sweet cinnamon scent. "Think of a sumo wrestler—massive, arms like a python—and he has a brother, Pasha. They're Russian. I'm meeting them at Josie's house at six. They'll get rid of those scum. You two stay here with Tasha."

"No way," says Josie. "I'm coming."

"Then I'm coming too," says Jordan.

"I'm not staying by myself," I say, clinging to Dom.

"You don't have to," says Dom. *"Okay, yous and yous."* He's broken into his awful rappa voice, and even Jordan's laughing out loud. *"Yous ma fam!"*

26. Josie

Just before six we leave Terry's Café and walk back to the house. I can feel the tension in Jordan's body as he holds me close, his arm around my waist. Am I scared? I don't know anymore. These past couple of weeks have been so mad, there's almost no point in being scared. The worst thing that can happen is me and Tash end up in care. I won't let Chaz touch her again and neither will Dom. We're certainly not going back into the house with Shirl and Bazza and their stupid knife.

Tasha whispered in my ear, just before we left the café, "I'm so glad Dom's finally got a girlfriend." But her eyes were glistening with tears.

I want to tell her how mad she is, that Dom's in love with *her.* It's so obvious. Why can't she see it? Something to talk about once we've sorted out the criminals.

As we stride along I say to Jordan, "If Dom's blokes can get rid of those two, maybe me and Tasha have a chance to find the money and pay Mum's debt."

"How much is it, Josie?"

"£5,466.42."

He gives a low whistle. Then he says, "I could ask my dad."

"No way!" That's all I need, another whole new debt, and to Hugo Prince, of all people. "Your dad doesn't even like me."

Jordan goes quiet, and his eyes disappear behind his cheekbones.

We turn into my street. I can see a white van and two men standing outside my house. Automatically I tell myself to walk past; we never open the door to anyone. But then I give a little inward laugh. Those days are long gone, Josie Tate. Everyone knows your business now.

Jordan stiffens as we arrive at the front door. He must really hate my house.

"This is Sasha and Pasha," says Dom, and he does some sort of stupid fist bump and finger wagging at them both.

Dom was right; sumo wrestler doesn't begin to describe Sasha. He's the biggest block of a human being I've ever seen, with his shaved head resting on massive shoulders and an even wider body. His legs are like tree trunks, and one of his hands could crush both of mine in a nanosecond.

Pasha is taller, over six feet, and although he's not so sumo he's still big, with muscles bulging under his clothes.

These two terrify me. What if they decide to take over after the crims have gone?

Then Sasha gives me this wonderful smile and says, "You need plumber? We the best." His voice is really, well, normal.

"Maybe later," says Dom.

"Okay, after we tell the nice peoples to leave," says Sasha.

Pasha stares at the front door, face grim, arms folded like a bouncer.

"I'm glad they're on our side," I murmur to Jordan.

He gives a worried nod.

Then Sasha thumps really hard on the door. It's like a thunderclap.

There are sounds from inside, and someone calls out, "Who's there?"

He nods to me and I say, "Josie. Forgot my key. Let me in."

More sounds, and then the door opens wide. For a minute I think I've got the wrong house. I can see down an almost-empty hallway. Where's Mum's collection? What have these two been doing?

Bazza is standing in the hallway with Shirl slightly behind him. I can see something pink in her hand. I take a step forward, but Jordan pulls me back.

"Who are your mates?" says Bazza.

Sasha says, "We come to send you away. Go now, please." His voice is still soft but it's edged with menace.

I see Shirl lift her hand, and there it is: the pink makeup bag. They've found the bankbook, and they're about to steal all my money!

"Right, that's it!" I say in a loud voice.

I slip free from Jordan, march up to the door and step into the hallway, holding out my hand. Having the Russian brothers here makes me feel like a giant. "Give me that," I say to Shirl.

There's a whoosh as the front door slams behind me, and then Bazza has grabbed me by the throat and Shirl's saying, "Call your army off, girly, or we'll slit you open and feed you to the birds."

How could I have been so stupid! I can hear Jordan and Tasha screaming and shouting outside. They're thumping and banging, but I can't hear the brothers.

Something cold presses on my cheek. It's Bazza's knife. I've had it now. He's pulling me back into the house. We're nearly at the stairs.

"We can get out through the kitchen window," Shirl says,

"now we've cleared a space and found what we're looking for." Her eyes are staring at me, but her cold lips are set in that horrid little grin. "It was tucked down the side of the oven, girly, all covered in rat droppings."

Eeugh!

She's waving the makeup bag in my face, and I try to lunge towards her. But Bazza grips me so tight I scream out.

Then there's the most almighty crash, and the front door smashes flat onto the hall floor, shaking all the windows.

Sasha's standing there and Pasha's looming over him. They look like everyone's worst nightmare. Their faces are set like concrete. I can feel Bazza shrivel behind me.

"Keep back!" he screams. "I'll finish her, I swear."

But Sasha strides up to us on his tree-trunk legs, and feeling that mass of muscle heaving in front of us makes even me feel nervous.

Bazza is literally shaking with fear. I swear I can hear his teeth rattling in his head, and a surge of triumph begins to build inside me. For the very first time since they forced their way into my life, these two are the ones who are scared.

Result!

The blade has begun to slip away from my cheek. Bazza's hand trembles as he stares at Sasha, who is baring his teeth.

How strange, I think. Why doesn't he just punch Bazza's lights out? Sasha frowns at me and jerks his head slightly and then I get it.

In one swift movement I drop my chin and bite down hard on Bazza's hand.

He lets out a yelp and drops his arm. With a roar, Sasha kicks out with his massive leg. The knife flies out of Bazza's hand and through the air. As I slither away, Pasha grabs me and pushes me out the door and into Jordan's arms. He grips me so tight I almost stop breathing.

Tasha and Dom are next to us. The screaming and yelling brings the students in the house next door out onto the street. They're laughing and cheering the brothers on.

Bazza appears in the doorway, held horizontal by Pasha, who's got one hand on his jacket and one on the belt of his jeans.

"Let me go, you bastard!" yells Bazza.

"Okay," says Pasha, who swings him twice in a great sweep and throws him so hard onto the pavement, he bounces.

Shirl follows, tossed out by Sasha like a bag of rubbish.

The students clap and cheer.

"You finished now," says Sasha in his quiet voice. "We say go please nicely, and you don't listen. Now you go very, very quickly."

Bazza and Shirl scramble up, clinging to each other, and stagger away down the street.

"Nice one," says one of the students, shaking Sasha's hand, and then they all go back into their house.

Pasha stands by the empty doorway, arms folded again, as if he's on guard.

Sasha says, "You see them again, call us. We have tell them what will happen if they return."

We all stand there in silence and then Dom says, "*Chai*?"

Tasha creases her eyebrows at him.

"It's Russian for *tea,*" says Dom.

"You have sugar?" says Sasha.

"Er, sure," I say, and everyone goes into the house and along the hallway.

I follow behind, and then I see Mum's picture—the cottage picture with the flowers and the slogan, *There's no place like home.* Someone's put it back on the wall. In the middle of the *o* in the word *home,* Bazza's knife is sticking out.

Jordan's waiting for me. "True justice," he says, and pulling the knife out, he wipes it clean on his jeans and places it in a box near the kitchen. "You could throw that out."

I could throw a lot out, I think.

We go upstairs, and Dom has tucked Tasha into my bed. Sasha and Pasha are standing behind the door. I grab the kettle, fill it, and then Tasha says in a small voice, "We can't sleep here tonight with the front door gone. It's scary."

"Sasha will fix it," says Dom in his soothing voice.

"What will it cost?" I say. I've got the makeup bag but I haven't had a chance to open it. I take it out of my jacket pocket now and stare at it.

Sasha and Pasha are muttering to each other. Then they give Dom a nod and a wink.

"Didn't Tasha say you've got some alcohol in the kitchen?" he says.

"Not sure," I say, trying to open the bag.

"Here," says Jordan, "let me have that." He takes the bag and starts fiddling with the zipper.

"There's boxes of booze," says Tasha.

"Sasha and Pasha could fix the front door for a couple of bottles of vodka," says Dom.

"Oh, sure," I say, and I give the brothers a big grin. "That would be amazing. Here, *chai.*"

I hand them the first two steaming mugs, and they pile in spoonfuls of sugar. We all start laughing and talking about Bazza and Shirl and how they fled like terrified mice.

"Josie big brave girl," says Sasha, smiling at me. "She take them on by her own."

"She's amazing," says Jordan.

"No, she's not!" says Dom. "You're crazy weird, Josie Tate. They could have killed you."

"Tell me about it," murmurs Tasha.

It's getting late, and Jordan says he has to go. "I got it open," he says, handing me the bag, and then we go downstairs and kiss good-bye.

Dom goes too, telling me to look after Tasha, which I promise to do.

The brothers get their tools out of their van and fix the door.

"We do new lock, Josie," says Sasha. "Here is key."

He stands there expectantly, and then I remember the vodka. I run back to the kitchen and grab four big bottles for them.

He and his brother exchange a few words in Russian, and then they say thank you and they're gone.

When I go back upstairs, Tasha's still awake.

"Are we safe?" she says in a weak voice.

"Totally. Dom wouldn't let anything happen to you."

She gives a little smile. "I know. He's my best friend."

"You're mad, Tasha," I say, and, ignoring the startled look on her face, I carry on. "Can't you see? He's crazy mad in love with you."

"Course he's not; he's going out with Freckly Emily. She's clever like him. I never do anything at school beyond the serious minimum."

"Yeah, well, I can't even swim, but that doesn't bother Jordan. I'm telling you, Dom is in love with you and..."

But she's fallen asleep and now I'm all alone in the silence of the house.

27. Josie

I need my own room again. I'm fed up with sharing, but Mum's room is in a disgusting state. The bed's covered with beer bottles, tins and half-full takeaway boxes, and the room stinks of the criminals.

There's no way I can sleep here tonight unless I clear up and open some windows. It's almost nine o'clock. I'd better get started, I think. Picking up two sacks behind the door, I take them to the top of the stairs and throw them down.

That feels good.

Once I start, I can't stop. I cart every single box and bag out of Mum's room and throw them downstairs. I can stack it all in the kitchen later and keep the hall clear. I can't bear the thought of filling it up again.

One of the sacks splits open, and there's brand new sheets, pillows and even a duvet with a new duvet cover still in its pack. I strip the bed down to the mattress and throw everything downstairs. Once I've cleared space around the windows, I manage to push one open, and the cold night air comes pouring in.

I can't remember the last time any outside air came into our stuffed-up house. It's past midnight and very quiet outside. There's a full moon in the sky, streaming in through the window and lighting up the bed. Now that I've started, I feel as though I'm on a mission to the stars. I can't stop until the house is empty.

As I sit on Mum's bed, clean with fresh sheets for the first time in months, I suddenly miss her so much. I know she hasn't made things easy, but she was always there for me, cuddling me as a little girl and helping me with my homework. I loved shopping with her in all the secondhand shops when I was a kid. It was like a continual treasure hunt, and she was so delighted with everything she found, like a child on Christmas Day every single day of the week.

I really do believe that our planet needs saving; I'm not just a brainwashed idiot. My mum has proper principles that she lives by. But I realize now from the TV program that it all went very wrong.

I think back to my last birthday. That was when she started saying, "Sixteen next year, Josie. I wonder where you'll be."

Does Mum think that I'll abandon her when I'm sixteen, like my so-called dad abandoned her and left her a single mum? She had Grandpa Ted, but he died two years later. Then she was all alone with me, this house and no money.

Does Mum think sixteen is the end of us living together, saving the planet, the Tates against the world?

Maybe that's why she let herself go, lost her job, stopped paying her bills and ignored the outside world until it came trampling in and put her in prison.

"Why didn't you talk to me, Mum?" I say out loud. Tears run down my face.

But I stop myself. I'm Josie Tate, and I don't have time for tears. I have to get my mum out of prison. She won't be home in time for my birthday on Thursday, but we can have our own special celebration later. I can wait.

Time to see if Grandpa Ted left me anything worth having.

I open the makeup bag and pull out a creased gray booklet. The cover says FIELDINGS MUTUAL BUILDING SOCIETY. They're on the High Street opposite the post office.

I open the book, and a sheet of paper falls out, all yellowed around the edges. It's a letter.

> Dear Josie,
>
> I know you won't remember me. I won't last much longer with my weak heart, and you're only two. But I wanted to leave you something to help you in the future. I had a win on the football pools, and so I've put the money into this account for you.
>
> Work hard at school and make your mum proud. She's a good girl really, she just had it tough.
>
> Love,
> Grandpa Ted

I open the pages of the savings book.

I can't believe my eyes.

Fifteen thousand pounds is entered in the savings column.

It can't be! I must be mistaken!

I flip back to the first page and there is my name, Josie Tate, and the date the account was opened. I'm rich!

I want to run out of the house straight away and go to the building society and take all the money out, but it's nearly two o'clock in the morning.

I fall asleep with the little gray book in my hand. When I

wake up, Tasha's shaking me and saying, "You'll be late for your paper route."

"I'm not going," I say in a blurry voice. "Look." I offer her the book.

Tasha takes it and opens it. *"Oh. My. God!* You're minted, babes! What you going to do with all that cash?"

"I haven't got it yet."

Tasha gives a laugh. "You soon will. Come on, get dressed. Breakfast's on me."

I pull on my jeans and a top. It's Wednesday morning. There's only me and Tasha in the house. I have to concentrate on getting Mum free.

"I'm not going into school today," I say to Tasha. "But you go—don't get into any trouble."

Tasha snorts and says, "Haven't got any use for school now that I'm homeless."

We fall silent. Tasha's got as many problems as me, hasn't she?

We have breakfast at the café, and then I say, "I'm off to the building society. What are you going to do?"

"I'm going to spring clean your bedroom, Josie, babes. Any more clean sheets anywhere?"

I give her a big grin. "I'm sure Mum has loads. Just keep opening sacks. But, Tasha."

"What?"

I grab her arm, suddenly scared. "Don't throw anything away. Mum wouldn't like it. Just stack it downstairs, promise?"

"Promise."

All the way to the building society, I imagine them handing the money over in a big bag, and then I'll catch the bus to the prison, pay the debt and they'll let Mum out. It's easy, I tell myself—won't take long.

It's already past nine, so the doors are wide open. I walk in and go up to the counter.

"Yes?" says the cashier.

I push the savings book under the glass. "I need to take out some of this money," I say.

The cashier takes the book and looks at it. Then she looks at me. "ID?" she says.

I push through my bus pass.

She looks at it and then says, "You're still fifteen, so you can't withdraw any money without an adult. You both need two pieces of ID: passport, driver's license, utilities bill..." She drones on and on with what sounds like an endless list.

I don't have any of those.

"Come back with your mother, and she can help you to sort it out, dear. Next, please."

"No, wait," I say, as a man behind me snorts impatiently. "Look, I'm sixteen tomorrow. Can't I just have a bit today? It's really important—it's for my mum."

The woman shrugs and says, "Come back tomorrow. But you need your birth certificate, and if you need more than one thousand..." She raises a querying eyebrow at me.

I nod and a single tear slips out of my eye and down my cheek.

"Then just ask your doctor for a letter verifying who you are." In a brisk tone, she looks beyond me and says, "Next, please."

The man behind shoulders me out of the way, and I stumble out of the bank.

Why does everything have to be *so* hard?

My phone rings. It's Jordan. I don't know what to do, and the ring tone drones on and on until I give in and press the button. "Hi," I say.

"Hey."

But my throat has closed up. I can't speak.

"Josie?" A worried tone has crept in. "You okay?"

"Sure," I say, gulping back a sob.

"You don't sound okay. What's up?"

Where do I start? Jordan doesn't even know it's my birthday tomorrow. I wanted to wait until Mum came home before celebrating. But I have to tell him something, so I mumble, "I'm sixteen tomorrow, and my mum's in prison."

"Oh," he says, and I can hear the disappointment in his voice. "Why didn't you tell me?" There's a silence, and then he says, "So, uh, do you wanna do something?"

"No, yes, maybe... All I want for my birthday is Mum home again." My voice breaks, and I can't hold back the tears.

"Sure you do, Josie. I get it."

Someone calls his name and he calls back, "Okay, okay.... Wait up."

Then his voice becomes more urgent as he says to me, "I have to get back, Josie. I'm competing today, and it's miles away. I won't be back till real late. Call you tomorrow, okay?"

"Okay," I say with a sniff.

He clicks off, and I'm alone again.

There's such an ache inside me, it feels unbearable. I walk off in a daze for what seems ages, and then I find myself outside Mel's pharmacy. There's a closed sign on the door, but it's midmorning. What does that mean?

I go to the flat and ring the bell. Footstep, patter down

the staircase, and the door opens a crack. “What is it?” snaps Mel.

I can’t hold the tears back any longer and then I’m sobbing and sobbing and Mel opens the door and pulls me inside.

Upstairs, Ivy’s lying on the sofa with her eyes closed. Len’s watching TV as usual. I gulp back my sobs, but neither of them seems to notice me.

“Grandma’s not feeling well today,” mutters Mel, glaring at me. “What’s the problem?”

It all spills out in one stream, and I finish by saying, “I’ve got my birth certificate—Mum keeps it in her jewelry drawer—but we don’t have a doctor, so how can I get that letter? I need my mum back home, Mel. I miss her so much.” More tears pour down my face. I try to mop them up with my sleeve.

“Hmm,” says Mel.

Len shifts in his chair and mutters to himself.

Then the doorbell rings. Everyone stiffens, and Ivy opens her eyes a crack.

I stare at Mel and she stares back.

“Doctor, for Grandma,” she says, and goes down to open the door.

I hear a woman speaking in a cheery voice as Mel brings her upstairs. The small room suddenly seems so full of people.

“Go and sit in the kitchen,” says Mel, flicking her head at me.

I leave the room and close the door. The murmur of voices comes through the wall. I have no idea what to do. It’s weeks and weeks before Mum’s out of prison.

“Josie, come in here.”

Mel’s calling me. I go back in the living room. The doctor’s still there.

Mel tells her about Mum and the debt and how it's my birthday tomorrow and I'm missing her so much. The doctor gives me a sympathetic smile. She has light brown skin and a red spot in the middle of her forehead. She's about Mum's age, and she's wearing a bright green top and black trousers.

"So what we need, Dr. Kumar," Mel finishes, "is a letter from you, please, to confirm Josie's identity."

Dr. Kumar stares at me for a few minutes and then she says, "Mel has talked to me about you before, Josie. I know she's been worried that you don't have a doctor."

I nod.

"I feel as though I already know you, and Mel tells me you're a good girl, supporting your mother and working hard at school." She raises a querying eyebrow at Mel and Mel gives a firm nod.

"I would be happy to write the letter."

Before I can say anything, Len yells, "Goal!" and everyone laughs.

The doctor sits down at Mel's dining table, takes out some headed notepaper—very posh-looking—writes for a few minutes, and then hands me the letter.

"That should do it. Your mother's very lucky to have such a resourceful daughter. I'm sure she appreciates you."

I manage to mumble my thanks, and the doctor pats me on the shoulder. Then Mel sees us both out.

I run all the way home. All I want to do is tell Tasha. How crazy weird is that?

28. Tasha

"Ta-dum!" I stretch out my hand like a TV presenter and wave Josie into her own bedroom.

"Wow, Tash! This is amazing."

I've managed to empty half the room and clear the window. I've thrown it wide open, and the morning sunshine's blazing in. I've found new sheets for the bed and a sweet Hello Kitty duvet cover.

"New pillows too." I say. "Your mum is quite a collector."

"Tell me about it," she groans. "Where's all the bags and boxes?"

"I've been really, really careful, Josie, honest. I've put things in the living room where you cleared all that space. The rest of it I've tidied up over on that side of the room."

I point to a stack of stuff almost waist-high that goes across the entire wall, covered now with a clean white sheet.

Josie nods with approval, and then she spots her desk. "Tash! You sorted out my books. Terrific. Oh, look at that cute pen pot!"

"Yeah, there's a ton of stationery in one of those bags for when you go back to school. . . ."

"If," she cuts in, shaking her head.

"No, Josie Tate, not if, when. You're a brainbox like Dom

and Freckly Em. You just need a bit of time to sort your head out."

Then she waves a piece of paper and says, "I got it!"

"What?"

She tells me all about the money and the doctor's letter, and I say, "All sorted, then."

I flop on the bed and grab a nail file. I found about a hundred in one of the sacks, and I need a serious manicure.

Josie gives a sigh and says, "Hopefully. Jordan rang. I told him I'm sixteen tomorrow."

"What did he say?"

"He's got another competition."

"Very romantic."

She gives a little laugh and then says, "Talk about romance, Jordan agrees."

I narrow my eyes at her.

"Dom's in love with you."

"Shut *up!* You're both insane. Dom just texted me to say he's meeting Emily today. They're working right through lunch together because she's stuck on her sums or something."

I've had such a funny feeling in my stomach since Dom's text. He's always been there for me; I sort of take him for granted. But somehow in the past week, my feelings have become all mixed up. I'm probably just jealous, aren't I?

"I'm glad that my sweet little Dom has found someone special," I say, filing away furiously at my nails. "He deserves it. Anyway, Emily's, you know..."

"What?"

"Geeky."

We burst into laughter, and then Josie says, "Wish I had a computer."

"You can use mine anytime." I grab my laptop and plonk it down on her desk. "Now you look like a proper brainbox. What else did Jordan say?"

"Nothing really." She stares out of the window.

I don't know what to say, so we're quiet for a while.

Josie turns on my laptop and starts surfing around. I finish tidying my nails and pull a dozen different varnishes out of a bag I found in the hoard. I choose a bright red as a base and then try out different colors on top in a pattern. I'm just beginning to think I could get a job in a nail bar when my phone goes. It's Mum.

I look over at Josie but she's glued to the screen.

I press the button and say, "Yep."

"How are you?" Her voice sounds as tight as mine.

"Yep," I say again.

"Chaz is away."

"So?"

"Let's have lunch, Tash. Time to sort things out, isn't it?"

I don't answer. I can feel my eyes welling up. What is she after? But I'm so missing my bed and my room and all my things. I really want to go home.

"Tash? Meet me during my lunch hour, the pizza place next to the post office. The flat's like a graveyard without your music on." She gives a little laugh.

I feel myself soften inside. She misses me. Maybe that means we can sort things out.

"Yeah, okay. Bye."

I click off and check my watch.

"I need a shower," I say.

Josie doesn't look up. "Hmm, okay."

I push a towel into my bag. It's a brand-new one I found in

the hoard along with a pack of new jeans, my size, black socks and three bras, one of which fits me. I choose new underwear and clean clothes and pack them with my shower stuff.

"I'm off to the pool, and then Mum wants to meet me for lunch," I say in a casual voice.

Josie's head jerks up. "And Chaz?"

"He's away."

"Okay, well, my phone's on and I can be with you real quick if you need me."

I nod and head out of the house, then catch the bus to the pool.

As I shower, get dressed and go back to High Street, I rehearse over and over what I'm going to say to Mum.

Chaz is a perv.

He likes young girls.

Why can't you see it?

Do you love me?

And a million other things, but nothing sounds right. By the time I get to the pizza place, my brain hurts. It feels like it's been stuffed inside one of the machines in the launderette and put on spin.

Mum's already at a table studying the menu. When she spots me she jumps up and grabs me in a bear hug. Then she pulls away and says, "Missed you." She lifts my hand and says with a laugh, "Love the nails!"

I shrug and sit down. "Might do a beauty course, open a nail bar."

"Hmm," she says, frowning. "You have to finish school first, and they've been on to me about you skipping off. What's going on?"

"I've been busy," I say. I've already decided not to tell her about my wound or Shirl and Bazza. I've pinned my hair over the dressing and it's quite hidden. She wasn't there for me, so what's the point?

"Okay," she says. "Let's order, and then we can discuss it."

We order pizza, salad, Coke and chips. I'm actually starving, and Mum says I can have anything I want. She's trying to make it up to me, I can tell.

"Here's some cash, get some new clothes." She grins and hands me a wad of notes. Three twenties. Brilliant.

I tuck them away in my jeans pocket and say, "Thanks."

There's something strange about the way she's looking at me. Chaz tried to give me money too, didn't he?

But then she starts to chatter on about work and I tell myself I'm getting paranoid. This is my mum; she's supposed to give me money and stuff.

"You remember Maddy in accounts?" Mum's saying.

I don't but I nod, my mouth fill of chips.

"Well, it was her bachelorette party last Saturday, so we all go out and get so drunk we have to call a cab to get home."

She's got such a stupid grin on her face, I blurt out, "What about Chaz? Couldn't he come and get you?"

"He was away." She chews for a minute and then she says, "You got him all wrong, Tasha."

"No, I haven't."

"Look, all I want to say is, I promise that if you come home and go back to school, I'll make sure you two are never alone again. I've put a lock on your door."

"Oh."

"That way Chaz can never get the wrong room again."

"No, I suppose not."

She looks at her watch. "I've got to go, Tash, but why don't you come to the house tomorrow evening. Chaz will be back. I'll make a nice roast and we'll all sit down together and sort things out. Will you, please?"

She looks so small and needy all of a sudden, I haven't the heart to blow her off. "Promise you'll listen to my side of the story?"

"Course."

"Okay," I say, and she gives me a hug, pays the bill and leaves.

I finish my meal, turning over in my mind all the things she said to me, looking for clues that she really loves me, that she wants me back home and that she will believe me about Chaz.

That's the unknown quantity, as Dom says. I have no idea if she and Chaz will listen and agree that I had a reason to be scared.

But if I don't show up tomorrow, does that mean I've left home forever and will never see Mum again?

That's too horrible to think about, so I decide I'll give it one more go.

As I walk away from the restaurant, my legs feel weak and my head's spinning again. I reach up and touch the wound through the dressing. It's throbbing away and feels very hot.

Is it a sign?

29. Josie

Thursday morning I wake up by eight and remember straight away.

Happy birthday, Josie, I think, and my eyes fill with tears. Mum's never, ever missed my birthday before. Then I spot a parcel on the end of my bed. It's from Tash. She must have sneaked in last night or very early this morning.

I open the present. It's a Hello Kitty bag bulging with all kinds of makeup. I can't help grinning and I get up and go down to Tasha's room. The door's open, and she's sound asleep. I don't want to disturb her. It's been such a rough week, and anyway I have a big job to do today.

I dress quickly, check my bag for the umpteenth time and go out of the house.

I rummaged through Mum's jewelry drawer again last night and found my birth certificate. It was all crumpled up at the back, and there's a massive tear across the middle. I stuck it back with sticky tape, but what if the building society won't accept it?

I keep checking my bag all the way to High Street in case the letter from the doctor drops out. My mouth's dry and my legs feel weak as I push open the door of Fieldings and go inside.

This is it, I tell myself. Go up to the cashier and ask for the money.

But I stop just inside the door. What if they say no? What if they send me away? What if . . . ?

I almost scream aloud, Just do it, Josie Tate! Don't think! The words thunder through my head, and then I make myself walk up to the counter.

"Can I help you?" says the cashier. She doesn't smile, but her face is neutral.

I push the savings book through with the birth certificate and the letter from the doctor. "I'm six—" My voice breaks.

The cashier stares at me.

I swallow and try again. "Uh . . . I mean . . . I'm sixteen today, and I want to take out some of this money."

There's an awful silence. The cashier looks at the savings book and then she turns over the birth certificate and the letter. She looks at them for ages with a frown on her face.

Then she says, "How much do you want to withdraw?"

"Five thousand, five hundred pounds," I mutter, and a sweat breaks out in my armpits at the sound of so much money.

The cashier's face is neutral again. She swivels in her chair and speaks to someone beside her. They give a nod, and then she turns back to me and says, "Just a minute, please."

My heart sinks. They won't give that much money to some kid like me. I'm wearing Mum's good coat again to try to look mature and responsible, but they're not fooled, are they?

A tall, thin man in a suit and tie appears and leans toward the cashier. They murmur together and nod. Then the man gives me a long stare. I drop my eyes and I feel myself going red all the way down my neck.

The cashier says, "That's a lot of money to take out. Wouldn't it be better to transfer it into your bank account?"

"No, I mean, you can't!" I blurt out, confused. "I need it

today and I don't have a bank account and Mum—I mean me—well, we have to pay the debt on the council tax today. It must be today. . . ." Tears well up in my eyes.

"Can't your mum come with you to get the money?" asks the thin man.

"She's in prison."

There's a silence, and then the man says in a softer voice, "I see. You want to pay the debt to get her released."

I nod.

He's murmuring with the cashier again, and then he says, "The money will be ready in five minutes, if you'd like to sit over there."

He nods toward some chairs, and I go and sit down before my legs completely collapse.

Then I'm walking down the High Street toward the council office, with over five grand in a bulging envelope in my bag, and there's only one more hurdle to leap before I set Mum free.

I can't stumble now; it's just not an option. But I'm shaking like a leaf and I almost wish crazy weird Tasha was with me, or even her sweet little Dom. But not Jordan—I'd be so embarrassed.

I go into the council building and walk past the receptionist, who doesn't even look up. My legs somehow keep pumping all the way down the long corridor to the Enquiries office.

The same woman is at her desk. She's tapping on a computer and without looking at me says, "Yes?"

I march up to the desk, slap my bag down, pull out the bulging envelope and tip fifty-pound notes all over her desk. They make a large pink mound, and the woman turns her head and stares at them and then stares up at me, her eyes wide with amazement.

"That money will pay my mum's council tax debt. I want

her out of prison because it's my sixteenth birthday today and I really, really miss her. . . ."

My voice breaks, my legs give way and I collapse in a chair, weeping quietly.

"Now, now," the woman says.

I mop my eyes with my sleeve.

Then I sit and watch as she carefully counts all the money. "I count £5,500.00," she says. "Did you rob a bank?" But there's a teasing smile around her lips.

"Grandpa left me the money." I hiccup between sobs and show her the savings book.

She nods and says, "I'll do what I can for you, dear." She pulls open a drawer and rifles around a bit, and then she holds out some money. "That's your change, £33.58."

I reach over and take it, and it feels good to have a bit of Grandpa's money in my hand.

"Now," says the woman briskly. "I have to make some phone calls, complete the forms and send a fax or two so that the court can authorize your mother's release. Let's hope we will have her home before the weekend. If you leave me your number, I'll call you as soon as I know anything."

I stare at her. I don't know what to think. But I have to trust her, don't I? I've done my best, and now I just have to wait. I print in large letters my phone number and full name and Mum's full name on a piece of paper, together with the name of the prison, so there can be no mistake. Then we say our good-byes. I say thank you at least three times so that she knows how grateful and desperate I am.

Outside the sun's shining and it's nearly eleven o'clock. I feel lost all of a sudden. I don't want to go to school, but there's nowhere else to go except home.

Then my phone rings. It's Jordan.

"Happy birthday, girlfriend. Ready for your surprise?"

I laugh so loud in some kind of relief that a man wobbles on his bike as he goes past. "What surprise?" I ask, and my voice ends in a kind of stupid shriek.

"Meet me at the pool at five and you'll see."

I can almost hear him grinning. For a moment I can't speak.

Jordan says, "Josie? You there? Will you meet me?"

"Sure," I say. "See you later."

He clicks off and I sprint to the bus stop as if I haven't a care in the world. I've paid the debt, Mum's coming home and Jordan wants to see me.

All the way home I turn over every single second of this morning. Maybe I'll start to measure my life in seconds too, just like Jordan does. I imagine the big clock at the pool, the huge black hand tick-ticking our lives out, second after second.

I love you Jordan Prince, I want to shout out loud.

Back home I stop and stare at the cottage picture still hanging on the wall, minus Bazza's knife. *There's no place like home.*

There's no place like my home, for sure, but for the first time in ages, I think, Maybe I'm not in such a hurry to move out.

Upstairs my coursework lies open on my neat and tidy desk. It's been so wonderful having Tasha's laptop, but she needs it back now. I decide to buy myself one with Grandpa's money. The thought of what I could do with that money makes me feel so grown up and independent. I could pay for some work around the house, maybe get a new stove. And then I have a brainwave and ring Dom to see if Sasha and Pasha will come by to help with clearing the house. I can afford to pay them properly now, not just in vodka. Then maybe we could do some decorating.

Mum will just have to agree to changes in the house. Butterflies still zoom around my stomach when I think of how she has always refused to even tidy up a little bit.

Stand up to her, I keep telling myself. Make it clear I won't live like this anymore. After all, I'm the one getting her out of that horrible prison, just like she begged me to in the letter.

She owes me.

Big time!

Then it's almost time to go out. I put on clean jeans and a green top with silver flecks to go meet Jordan. He told me to bring my swim stuff, so what's so special about that?

When I arrive at the pool, he's already waiting outside. "Your limo, ma'am," he says, opening the door of a cab.

We cuddle up on the backseat, and the cab drives us around the edge of town until I can see the hills in the distance, the same hills in the view from Jordan's house. Minutes later we turn onto his road.

"Are we going to your house?" I say, a chill going through me.

"No way," he says.

The cab whizzes past and on to a house much farther down the road. Jordan pays and we get out.

It's another gated palace. Jordan goes up and punches the keypad. The gate swings open.

"We're breaking into the neighbors'?" I say.

"They're friends of ours," says Jordan, grabbing my hand and pulling me along the path. "They're away at the moment, but they give us the codes."

We go around the house, and a single-story building

stretches across the enormous back lawn. The walls on both sides are almost entirely glass.

"This way," says Jordan, going up to a door on the side and punching another keypad.

Then he turns to me and says, "Close your eyes, Josie. Trust me, this is the best birthday present you ever had."

A thrill goes through me, and I close my eyes. Jordan takes my hand. I hear the door open, and we go through. I can feel warm air on my face, and then Jordan says, "Open now."

"Wow!"

I can't believe it. A swimming pool, with underwater lights that flow from green to red, stretches out before me. Wide steps lead down into the water, and around the pool are sun loungers with great soft cushions. I stare out of the glass wall to the line of hills in the distance, fading in the sunset.

Then a stab of fear goes through me. "Jordan, it's beautiful, but we should go before someone catches us."

He laughs and says, "No one's around, and anyway, I'm allowed to swim here whenever I want."

"Amazing."

"Go and change, and I'll meet you in the water."

He waves toward a door. When I go through, I see a small changing room with two showers and proper hair dryers. Paradise.

Tasha would love it here, I think. I know how much she's missing home comforts.

I check my phone. Nothing from her. She must be with her mum. Maybe the horrible Chaz has disappeared, so they can make up properly. She might even stay the night.

Then I don't think about Tasha again as I go out and into the pool, which is almost bath warm. Floating about, watching

Jordan zip up and down, I feel like a rich princess with my prince.

Jordan swims up to me, and then he ducks under the water and comes up, lifting me onto his shoulders.

I shriek as he piggybacks me up and down the shallow end, then lets me down gently.

We stand facing each other, up to our waists in the warm water, as a sort of confused glow whips through me. I feel myself go red and flush all the way down my neck.

His eyes have retreated too, like they do when he's thinking too much, and then he says, "Today you are going to swim completely alone."

"In your dreams," I say, laughing out loud.

But he pushes and cajoles and encourages me as I lunge around, trying to move in the water without my feet touching the bottom. Just when I feel like giving up, something connects between my legs and my brain, and suddenly I'm horizontal in the water, moving my arms and legs to a rhythm. I can't believe it! I'm actually swimming—but it's a long way to the other end.

Jordan's yelling, "That's it! Keep going, come on! All the way down the length! You can do it! Move those arms, breathe..."

I roll and kick and push my arms, and when I look up I can see the end. I strain my fingers to full stretch until they ache, and finally I touch the wall. I've done it! A whole length on my own. It's the most fantastic feeling in the world.

"Olympic gold to Josie Tate!" Jordan calls out.

I come upright, wiping the water from my face. Jordan grabs me and we jump up and down, laughing in each other's arms. Then we're kissing until we run out of breath.

"Best day of my life, ever," I say.

“Me too,” says Jordan. “Fish and chips?”

“Sure.”

“See you out front in ten.”

As I go into my own gleaming, private changing room, I feel as though my life is beginning to change forever.

30. Tasha

I let myself into the flat and stand inside the front door, listening. It's five thirty, and Mum should be home from work.

"Tash? Is that you? Only me at home."

No Chaz, I think with mega relief.

I go down the corridor and say, "Hi."

Mum's chopping vegetables, and there's delicious smells coming from the oven.

"Chaz has been held up. We'll have dinner without him. He'll be back later."

My heart sinks again. No escape.

"Okay," I say, "I'll go down to my room."

She gives me a smile and goes back to chopping.

It feels strange opening my bedroom door after all this time. There's thick dust on my bedside lamp and table, the bed's all crumpled, just how I left it when I ran away from Chaz, and Dad's photo has slipped in its frame. I don't think Mum's been in here since I went.

I thought she might have wanted to make it all clean and bright for me if she really wanted me to move back home.

Is it another sign?

I pick up Dad's photo, unzip my backpack and slip it inside, next to Mickey. I don't leave home without Mickey these days. I never know where I'm going to end up.

The wound in my head throbs, and I feel so hot. Am I safe at home? If not, where do I go next? It won't be long before Josie springs her mum from prison and those two go back to being cozy little Mum and daughter like Mum and me never were, if I'm honest.

These past couple of weeks have made me realize that I might have a nice clean home and all the *things* I want—iPhone, laptop, makeup, pocket money, clothes, etc., etc.—but unlike everyone in all the sleepovers I've done—Shazia, Tansy, Dom and even Josie—my mum's not really there for me.

"Come and set the table," Mum calls out as if I've never been away.

I go into the kitchen and lay two places.

"Lay one for Chaz. He might make it before pudding."

I stare at her for a second or two. She meets my eye and then turns away. I thought maybe she was going to say sorry. I give an inward snort. No sign of that.

Dinner's wonderful. The best meal I've had since I walked out. Roast chicken, roast potatoes, Yorkshire puddings, and three kinds of veg.

"I've got a cake for after," says Mum.

I can see she's trying, so I smile and say, "Terrific."

She asks me about school. I tell her the lies she wants to hear, that I go in every day and I'm doing all my homework. She's easily satisfied, doesn't quiz me like a proper mother would do. Dom's mum would ask.... But there's no point, is there? You only get one mum, and this is mine—Heather Brown, nearly forty-four and desperate.

"So what about Chaz?" I cut into a story she's telling me about the girls in the office.

"What do you mean?" Her eyes narrow as she starts to collect the plates.

This is the talk I thought we were going to have, but I realize she always knew that Chaz would be late and had no intention of facing up to anything.

The wound stabs in my head, and I feel myself get hotter and hotter. It feels like a furnace in the flat. For a few seconds the room spins.

"You know what I mean, Mum. Don't you want me back home?"

"Don't make me choose, Tasha. It's not fair. Chaz and me are good together, and like he says, you need to grow up and accept it."

"Oh, so Chaz decides our lives now."

There's the sound of a key in the lock and the front door opening. Mum and I freeze. I stare at her, eyes wide. She stares back, and then she smooths down her skirt, pats her hair and goes into a sickening, simpering pose as Chaz appears in the doorway.

"Missed you, lover!" He strides over, grabs her and locks her in a revolting kiss.

Then he puts her down and turns to me. "The long-lost daughter comes home."

His tone is cruel and mocking.

I hate you, I hate you, floats around and around my aching head.

But I have to try, I tell myself. He hasn't done anything to me. Yet.

Mum dishes up dinner for Chaz and cake for us. I just push it around my plate.

Mum and Chaz chatter away, and then something crazy weird happens.

Chaz turns to me and says, "Tasha, me and your Mum, we really missed you, didn't we, Hev?"

She nods and smiles at me.

"All I want to say is, I'm sorry if we had a misunderstanding. If you move back in, I'll tread on eggshells. I said so, didn't I, Hev?"

Mum nods. "He did, Tasha—been saying it all week."

"And your mum's put a bolt on your bedroom door. You're a big girl now, nearly sixteen, right? You need your privacy. So, what do you say?"

I stare at him, and honestly, he looks and sounds just like the old Chaz, weeks ago before all the funny business, when I was planning to be a goth bridesmaid at their wedding and he took us out to the fair for a treat.

You can get people wrong, sometimes, can't you? Maybe I was wrong. After all, if he really wanted to do something to me, he would have found me. This is only a small town. Difficult to hide for long.

I'm so tired and my head's aching so much. It would be so good to go into my room and into my own little bed with Mickey and sleep and sleep. I'd be safe with the new bolt. I've already tried it out; no one could get through that.

I nod and say, "Okay, I'll give it one more try."

"That's my girl," says Chaz.

Mum comes around the table and gives me a hug. For a minute I rest on her big bosoms and wish I could stay like that, safe and warm forever.

Chaz finishes dinner and goes off into the living room to watch the match. Mum shoos me away. I think of going and watching TV, but something stops me. Plenty of time for that if things work out, I tell myself.

I go into my room, push the bolt in, sit on my bed and check my phone. There's a text from Dom. His mum's sick again, and he's got to look after his little brothers. They've had him up since five, he's behind in his homework and he's shattered.

Poor little Dom.

I send a text to Josie. *Staying with Mum. See you at the weekend.*

She texts back a few minutes later. *Great. On a super date with Jordan.*

Super! Who says that? She's as bad as Dom with his awful rappa stuff. I can't help grinning. If I had my laptop, I'd do a vlog. Make a record for the future, or whatever, about moving back home.

Only I'm not sure about it yet. One night at a time, I tell myself.

So far so good. Its nearly ten, and no one's been rattling my door.

I'm too tired to brush my teeth, so I just get into my pajamas—i.e., tracksuit bottoms and sweatshirt—cuddle Mickey close to my heart, and pull the duvet over my head. I sleep like the dead.

I wake up to the sound of someone knocking on my bedroom door. "Tash?"

Oh God! It's HIM! My bones freeze as I clutch Mickey.

But no one rattles the door, and then Chaz calls out again, "Your mum says get dressed. She's making you bacon and eggs for breakfast. Bathroom's free—I'll be in the kitchen."

I hear his footsteps go down the corridor, and everything goes quiet.

It's seven on my alarm clock. I'm in my own bed, in my own room, and Chaz is behaving like, well, like he always used to. It's as though I dreamed the past couple of weeks, him coming on to me and sleeping in the filthy old hoarder house with no bathroom.

All I have to do now is grab a towel and walk to the shower. As hot water pours over me, I feel the plaster loosen from my wound. I pull it away and dump it in the bin. The wound feels lumpy and hot, but there's no blood.

Back in my room, I dig out clean clothes and pull on my trusty boots. At least they haven't got holes like Josie's shoes. Now she's got some money, hopefully she'll buy an entire new wardrobe. We could go shopping together. I grin at the thought.

I turn my ankles and admire the steel tips on my boots, the ones my form teacher threatened to remove with a screwdriver if I wore them to school again. It's all about not getting caught, I'm always telling Dom. He never breaks the rules, does my little Dom. I wonder how things are at home for him, trying to make breakfast for his annoying brothers as his mum's sick in bed.

I could offer to go over and help. Then I think, no, that's Freckly Emily's place now. She's his girlfriend. For some reason, tears well up in my eyes.

I brush them away and go and push back the bolt. When I open the door, I let out a gasp.

Chaz is standing there, so close he's almost touching me, and he has his finger to his lips.

The thought that it's a joke flashes across my mind.

Then he lowers his finger and strokes my cheek with it just

like last time. "I'm so glad you changed your mind, Tash," he breathes.

He drops his hand onto my shoulder and it feels like a vise and he's pushing me backward into my room.

"No!" I scream out, and Mum puts her head around the kitchen doorway. "Get your hands off me!"

Instantly his face changes, all teeth and stinking hot breath on my face, as he says in a loud voice, "You little bitch! I didn't do nothing, Hev, honest."

"Mum! He…he…" Words fail me as I see Mum come down the corridor.

The look on her face is even more ferocious than Chaz's. As he steps to one side, her hand swings and a slap smacks across my face like an electric shock.

I scream and stagger across the doorway. No one catches me, and my shoulder slams into the frame, making me cry out again.

My bag! Mickey! I turn, rush into my room, grab my stuff, and, pushing Chaz with all my strength, I run to the front door, down the staircase and out to the street.

I turn and look behind me, but there's no one there.

I could hear Mum crying as I ran and Chaz saying, "She just came back to get money out of you."

I can't believe it. He's taken over her life, and she's like some sort of zombie with him. I don't matter to her one little bit. It's like she's rubbed me from her life with that Hello Kitty eraser I found for Josie's desk.

As I stumble off in the rain, my cheek stinging and my shoulder aching, the wound starts to throb again. It's freezing outside, and I forgot my jacket. But it doesn't matter. I feel like

I'm in a furnace again. My wound is keeping me hot like my mother can't be bothered to do.

I turn onto High Street and there's the launderette, warm and cozy with the washing turning and turning, going into a spin like my head, scooping me into its dream world.

I sit there until I lose all track of time and night falls outside the door.

Then a dog is growling and sniffing around my feet, and looking up I see the man with keys glaring down at me again. "I told you before, you little cow. No homeless in here."

My mouth's too dry to speak, so I pick up my backpack and go out into the street.

Then everything goes dark.

31. Josie

Sasha and Pasha turn up at ten on Friday morning and start to clear the kitchen. I can't help feeling nervous as they pull sacks and boxes out of the front door, but I tell myself Mum will just have to accept it. Hopefully after two weeks in a nice clean empty cell, she'll hate the hoard as much as me when she comes home. I've been checking my phone every second to see if there's a message from the council or even the prison.

The van's filling up, and I'm heaving a black sack into the back when I feel a light touch on my shoulder.

"Here, let me help." It's Jordan, and he takes the sack from me and throws it into the van. "Where's this lot going?"

"The dump," I say. But I'm so on edge I drop a bottle on the floor and it smashes open.

"Hey, chill," says Jordan. "What's got into you?"

I shrug and say nothing. Mum might not get out for days yet, so there's no point telling him.

We form a chain down the hallway, with Pasha in the kitchen, me and Jordan in the middle and Sasha on the street throwing stuff into the van.

"Cooker," says Pasha, stopping to wipe his forehead.

I go into the kitchen and there it is, covered in dirt and grease. Jordan comes up behind me, looking really disgusted.

"How much is a new one?" I say.

"Maybe two hundred and fifty. Sasha know good place to buy."

I add it to my mental list, along with a new shower, sink, toilet and about a million other things.

"Won't take long to spend Grandpa's money," I say to Jordan. "I don't think there'll be anything left over for college."

"I could ask my dad about investments and stuff."

I shake my head. Not Jordan's dad, no way. I start pulling out another sack. Then there's a shout from the street and a woman's voice.

It can't be!

I run down the corridor, Jordan following behind me. Sasha's standing by his van, arms folded, and there's Mum!

I scream and throw myself at her and we hug for what seems ages. Then she pulls back and for a minute I almost don't recognize her. She's cut her hair to about one inch long all over and dyed it white blond. It looks horrendous.

Her eyes are ringed with dark patches, almost like bruises. She felt so thin when we hugged, I swear I could feel her ribs through her jacket, and there's a funny smell about her. But she's my mum, and she's home.

Then she says in this weird hoarse voice, "What are they doing, Josie? What's been going on here?"

This is it, I think, and I say, "We're doing a bit of a clear out, Mum—you know, like we always said we would one day."

"Clear out?" Her eyes narrow and her voice has gone down a level. "Behind my back? Who do you think you are, you little madam, bringing people into my house, going through my precious collection—"

"But, Mum, we can't go on living like this.... You know

we ca…" My voice peters out as Mum launches herself into the back of the van.

She starts tearing away at sacks and boxes, throwing them onto the street, ranting away like a lunatic the whole time. "I go away for just two weeks, and look what you do! Who are these people? Get them out of my house. You!"

She points at Sasha, "Put everything, and I mean everything, back exactly where you found it!"

Sasha shrugs and looks at me.

"And you!"

She points at Jordan. Oh God! Then she yells, "Take this inside!" and without any warning she's thrown a box straight at him. It hits his right arm and he gives a huge yelp of pain.

"Jordan! Let me see," I say, my voice shaking with anger and the utter embarrassment of it all. But he shoulders me away, gripping his bad arm.

I stumble back, eyes welling with tears.

Mum's still yelling, "Get out of my house and out of my street!"

"MUM!" I shriek back, and suddenly we're yelling and screaming at each other like two cats in an alleyway.

Jordan shakes his head and, still holding his bad arm, his face dark with anger, he turns and runs down the street and around the corner.

I stand there staring after him, shocked into silence, while Mum kicks and pushes and throws all the stuff from the van onto the street. I'll never see him again! Some of the bags split open and leak stuff into the gutter—plastic bottles, a broken clock, fluffy toys, all the useless stuff that Mum can't bear to be without.

Then she jumps down from the van and pushes Sasha like

he's an old workhorse or something. "You're not wanted here anymore," she snarls.

Sasha shouts to Pasha in Russian and they shut the back doors of the van, climb in and drive away.

No one has said good-bye to me.

I stand on the street, tears pouring down my face, while Mum grabs and heaves sacks and boxes back into the hall, just when we had cleared a proper space. She has driven everyone away, just like she's always kept other people away from us.

I was desperate for Mum to come home, but she's ruined my life all over again. She's driven away my gorgeous, kind, thoughtful boyfriend and wrecked my hopes of clearing the house so we can invite friends over. Prison hasn't changed her one little bit, except for the worst.

As I listen to Mum ranting and raving about her stupid hoard, I can almost hear Tasha say in her bored voice, "Crazy weird, or what?"

I'm done here, I think, and a weakness spreads through my body. I could flop down like a puppet onto the pavement right now.

I force myself to move, push past Mum and go up to my bedroom. I take one last look at how sweet and clean Tasha has made it for me. Then I stuff a few clothes into my school back-pack, grab my purse, pull on my jacket and walk downstairs.

Mum's in the kitchen ranting to herself. "Everything's been moved around. I'll have to work all night to put this straight...."

She turns on me and yells, "Have you no respect? You know our rules; no one even looks through our front door!"

I turn my back on her and walk out of the open door and into the street. Her voice fades as I walk away from her and my life forever.

No more Jordan, no more Tasha and her sweet little Dom, no more Sasha and Pasha, no more Angel doing my hair. I'm not someone who has friends and boyfriends. Not with a mother like mine.

I hesitate at the corner. I have no idea where to go.

What about Mel? Maybe she'll let me sleep on her floor for a few days until I decide what to do next.

I walk along the street to the pharmacy. There's a closed sign, so I knock on Mel's front door. No answer. I ring the bell.

"They're gone." It's the pet shop man, and he's got a nasty leer on his face.

"Where?"

"The Social came, winkled them out like I knew they would. Took them away this morning. Mel's gone with them."

He goes back into his flat and shuts the door, leaving me alone on the pavement.

No one's safe at home, I think. They've run Ivy and Len to ground and grabbed them out of their hidey hole.

And what about me? I'm homeless now, just what Tasha was always terrified of. In the end, it's me who'll sleep in a doorway tonight.

It starts to rain again like it has on and off for weeks, since the night of the storm when Tasha turned up on my doorstep.

Where do homeless people go when it's raining?

I walk off without thinking where for what seems hours. Finally, I see the lights of a café up ahead. I'm in a rough part of town that Mum warns me to stay away from. But what does it matter anymore? No one cares where I go. This is probably the right place for someone like me.

I go into the café, buy a chipped mug of tea at the counter and sit down at a table in the window. Now what, Josie Tate?

I stare out of the window in a daze for hours as the light fades and it becomes dark outside. The café empties around me, and then someone says, "Got a light?"

A boy's standing over me. His face and hands are covered with tattoos and he has rings through his nose, bottom lip and both eyebrows.

I hear a high-pitched giggle behind him and some muttering. He looks over his shoulder at a group of three boys and two girls lounging at a table in the corner. They're all tattooed and pierced, and they look so creepy they make me shudder.

The boy looks back at me and forces his lopsided mouth into a grin. "Ignore them dozy clowns."

His voice is hoarse, and his eyes don't seem to focus properly. He jerks his unlit cigarette toward me.

I shake my head. "I don't smoke, sorry."

My voice sounds posh in this dump. The clock on the wall says ten, and the owner's beginning to close up.

The boy slopes off back to his group. They're all leaning over each other, looking at me. I try not to stare back as a deep chill goes through me.

Time to leave, I tell myself, but as I stand up the group moves swiftly forward and the boy stands in the doorway.

"Come with us to a party." He's almost slurring his words. They're on drink or drugs or something. Is this what happens on the streets?

You get raped. End of. Tasha's words about becoming homeless come back to me.

I have to escape, and with a sudden move, I wrench the boy's arm forward and past me so he falls into his dozy mates. Then I race out the door.

I hear yells behind me as I zigzag across the road and down

a back alley. The rain's falling hard, so I have to keep wiping my face. Then I stumble, and my backpack slips off my shoulder. I can hear the boy yelling behind me, "I'll kill her!"

No time to stop for my pack. I keep running and running, dodging down one alley and then another. Just as I think I can't run anymore, I see some huge bins behind a takeaway shop. They stink worse than Mum's cooker at home, but I have no choice. I can hear voices only seconds behind me, almost in this alleyway.

I lift the lid, heave myself in and sink into squelchy rubbish as the lid shuts above me. I cower down and cram my hand into my mouth to stop screaming.

32.

Footsteps come nearer and nearer and stop right near my bin. Someone says, "She's gone. Let's go—we've got her bag."

There are mutterings and grumblings, but eventually I hear them walk away.

Everything goes silent. I'm covered in moldy half-eaten food; it's in my hair, behind my ears, all over my face, everywhere. They've stolen my bag with my clothes, my money, even my door key, and I'm stuck in a bin in the worst part of town. I don't even have the bankbook with me to get some money out in the morning. I put it under my mattress to keep it safe and didn't think to take it with me when I walked off. How stupid is that?

I fumble in my pocket for my phone, but it's not there. Then I remember; I left it charging on my bedside table. I can't ring someone for help even if I wanted to. But there isn't anyone, is there?

Jordan must hate me so much now that he's seen my crazy mum. Maybe his arm's damaged and she's ruined his chances at Olympic gold. He'll never speak to me again. I don't blame him.

What's the point of going on? What's the point of anything? Might as well throw myself off a tower block.

I stay like that for what seems ages, and then there's a small rustling sound near my feet and something runs up my leg. I can feel a tapping through my jeans and then I realize it's a rat!

It's as though I've been kicked from behind. I lunge upward, push the lid back with a crash and leap out of the bin. The rat flies off my leg and scurries down the alleyway. My stomach heaves. I lean over and vomit until tears run down my face.

I can't stay here. I'm terrified the gang will come back and kill me.

I brush off as much of the food bits as possible from my clothes and hair, shove my filthy hands in my pockets and trudge off through the rain. If I freeze to death tonight, at least I'll be in the open and under the pure white moon and stars, crisp and clean like Nariko's carpet and untouched by human filth.

I walk and walk until I see the light of a fire in front of what looks like a derelict building. There are a few people sitting and standing around. Some are lying on the ground in sleeping bags, but there's no sign of the boy and his gang. These people are older, and there's a couple of women. There's a stone to one side and I slump down on it facing the fire. No one takes any notice of me, which is a relief.

Then someone comes up and I flinch, but they take my hand and push a steaming paper cup of soup in it. "Just drink that. Don't need to say anything, love," says a woman's voice.

I don't look up, I don't trust anyone out here, but as she moves away I peek out of the corner of my eye. She's warmly dressed and she doesn't look like the down-and-outs, the homeless and the lost like me. She walks up to a van where there are others also handing out food.

I sip the soup and listen to the hum of voices around the

fire. One old bloke with hair all over his face and ragged clothes starts a loud argument with a woman.

"It's all the government's fault!" he shouts.

He sways on his feet as if he's drunk and swigs from a plastic bottle. The woman pushes him away, cursing in a high-pitched voice.

There's a slamming of doors. The soup people climb in the front of the van and drive off. I feel so alone again.

It must be really late, maybe two or three o'clock in the morning. All the warmth from the soup cup has gone. I'm so cold, I don't want to move away from the fire, but I don't want to stay here with the tramps.

"Where's your cardboard?" A voice comes out of the dark behind me.

I turn and look up. It's a girl, older than me, long stringy hair and a thin face, with a huge bag on one shoulder. Under the other arm she's carrying a sheet of cardboard.

I shrug and turn away.

"Mocha," she says in a more friendly voice.

I turn back. "What?" I say, confused.

"Mocha's me street name," she says. "What's yours?"

"I'm Josie," I say, and the girl hunkers down in front of me.

"Newbie," she says with a snort. "No one gives their real name on the street. I've got enough for two if you wanna share." She nods at the sheet of cardboard under her arm.

I shake my head. I don't want to fall asleep with the drunken man tripping over me.

"Not here with that pile of crones." Mocha jerks her head toward the people around the fire.

"Where then?"

"Follow me." She stands up and walks off toward the road.

I hesitate, and then I think, Might as well. I get up and follow Mocha, who's striding away, bent under her enormous bag.

"I can take the cardboard," I say, and she lets me slip it from under her arm.

We walk on in silence until we reach a parade of shops. "Down here," says Mocha, and we go into an alleyway. "It's usually dry, and no one will disturb us."

That sounds good. I've already learned that the last thing you want on the streets is other people.

So why trust this Mocha chick? comes Tasha's voice in my ear.

What choice do I have? I ask myself as Mocha drops her bag halfway up the alley. "Here," she says.

She's right; it is dry and doesn't smell too bad.

I lay down the cardboard and Mocha unzips her bag and pulls out a sleeping bag and a blanket. She throws me the blanket. "Don't have any stuff, do you?" she says.

"Lost it," I say. "Thanks."

Mocha lays out her sleeping bag. She crawls in, pulls the top over her head and zips up until only her face is showing.

I drop down on the cardboard and roll myself in the blanket, and although it's not exactly warm, for the first time since I drank the soup I actually stop shivering.

"Safer to buddy up on the streets," says Mocha. "How long you been out?"

I lie there in silence for a minute, Tasha's voice in my ear warning me not to give anything away.

I'm used to keeping secrets with a mother like mine. But then I get a terrible pang as I think of Mum and how much I missed her when she was in prison. I was so looking forward to her coming home and having little cozy chats on the bed again.

I was certain she'd be so pleased that I'd finally started to clear up. Why did she react in that horrible way?

And what about Jordan? But I don't want to think about him right now, so I mutter, "I left yesterday afternoon."

"First week's the worst," says Mocha. "I've been on the streets for two years, since I was fifteen. Take my advice: keep clear of the mental cases."

"How do you survive?" Two years. I can't imagine it.

"Just do. I was in the hospital last month for a week. Pneumonia. One day they just told me to go home."

"So why didn't you?"

"Mum's dead and Dad's dead drunk, likes to use his fists on me. I'm safer on the streets. What about you?"

But I don't want to tell her about Mum, so I say, "Same."

"Parents," says Mocha with a snort, and then there's just the sound of snoring.

I'll never fall asleep, I tell myself, but then someone's shaking me and it's daylight. My mouth's dry and I feel as if I haven't washed for months.

Mocha's on her feet, stuffing her sleeping bag in her huge hold-all.

I stand up, fold the blanket and hand it to her. "Thanks," I say.

"No worries. Breakfast?"

"Haven't got any money."

"There's a place in a church I know."

She takes off down the alleyway, and I pick up the cardboard and fold it under my arm.

As I turn onto the street, Mocha's waiting for me. "Drop that and let's move. Come on," she hisses.

She's looking nervously over her shoulder, which is a bit strange. But maybe she's seen one of her "mental" cases.

I spot a litter bin and prop the cardboard neatly next to it. There's an old man nearby, leaning on a walking stick, rummaging in his jacket pocket, a bewildered look on his face.

I'm about to ask him if he's okay when Mocha grabs my arm, pulls me down the street and into a café.

"Full English?" she says, brandishing a wallet with five-pound notes sticking up.

I stare at her, confused. "Where did you get that?"

"It was just lying on the pavement. Finders keepers."

"What? No, it's not," I say. "Didn't you see that old man looking in his pockets? What if that's *his* money?"

She shrugs. "We all gotta survive. I'm hungry, you're hungry, we're sleeping rough, we need it more than him."

"No way, Mocha. I'd rather starve."

Her eyes widen and for a second they are filled with such sadness, and then they narrow. "I didn't steal nothing; I'm not like that. But it's hard on the streets, Josie. You'll find out soon enough."

My heart goes out to her and I almost give in, but I pull myself together and say in a low voice, "Give me the wallet."

Mocha stares at me as if I'm mad.

"Give it to me or I'll call the police."

She lets out a sigh, and her shoulders sag like a deflated balloon. Then she drops the wallet on the table, picks up her bag and walks out of the café, her thin body stooped under the weight of her stuff.

I pick up the wallet and open it. Inside there's a photo of an old couple smiling. I walk out of the café and stare at the man. It's definitely him. He's still searching his jacket pockets.

I take a deep breath and walk up to him. "Excuse me, sir. I found this on the pavement. Is it yours?"

A look of utter relief crosses his face. "Yes, oh yes, oh what a good girl! I'd just taken out twenty pounds for the shopping, and what would I have said to my wife?" Then he reaches into a pocket, takes out a two-pound coin and presses it into my hand. "For your honesty," he says.

I stand in the middle of the pavement as he walks off, his stick tapping away. I'm staring at the coin in my palm and it's almost as if it's shouting at me, Wake up, Josie Tate! What do you think you're doing?

Why am I sleeping rough and hanging out with some homeless girl who hates old people and thinks she can keep anything she finds on the streets? I think of Ivy and Len and how sweet they are, and how I wished they could be my grandparents. Maybe Mocha has never really met any nice old people.

Is that the kind of person you want to turn into, Josie Tate?

That café had a toilet, I remember. I'll go back, get tea and toast with the old man's money, and then go to the toilet, clean myself up as best I can and go home.

Home! Just the word puts a spring in my step. Whatever is up ahead for me and Mum, I don't belong out here. I have a roof over my head, not like Mocha. I hate the fact she wanted to keep the old man's money, but I can't help feeling sorry for her. She's been on the streets for years, and she really has nowhere to go.

But that's not me.

If things don't work out at home, then I'll move out. I've still got Grandpa's money. But until then, I need a safe place to put my head down. Otherwise I'll end up like Mocha and the old people around the fire.

33.

It's midmorning by the time I arrive home. I rap hard on the front door and rattle the mail slot, but no one comes. For a minute I don't get it. I've become so used to millions of people arriving at my front door in the past two weeks and coming in and out as if that was the most normal thing in the world.

But Mum never opens the door, and I can't ring her. My phone's in my bedroom.

I bend down, push open the mail slot and call through, "Mum! It's me! Open the door."

I call until I'm hoarse, and just when I'm about to give up, the door opens and Mum hisses, "Come in, quick!"

I skip through the front door and she slams it shut behind me. Then she bursts into tears and grabs me, yelling, "Where have you been? I've been so scared. I rang your phone and then I heard it in your bedroom. What's going on?"

She pauses for breath. I stand there, enjoying her arms holding me tight, and then she says, "You know I needed help to put the collection back."

It's like she's set a bomb off under me.

I push her away and scream, "You what? Are you completely insane?"

Mum stands there staring at me. I nearly walk out again but the anger inside me is bursting out.

"You haven't missed me at all, have you?"

"You know that's not true Josie," Mum says, and she turns away as if we're finished.

I grab her arm and turn her back to face me. I have to get through to her or what future do we have together? "Just listen for once!" I yell back. "The only thing that really matters to you is your STUPID collection! You just want me to go along with your plans while you bury my entire life under a mound of... of... complete and utter RUBBISH!!"

"You can't say that—"

"I'll say whatever I like. I thought you'd be pleased I'd started to clear up. I thought you'd be pleased I got you out of prison with Grandpa's money. I thought prison would change you. It hasn't! Not one little, teeny-weeny bit. Well, as far as I'm concerned, you're on your own now. You can have your disgusting stuff; I'm leaving!"

I'm so tired after my horrible time on the streets with almost nothing to eat for two days, and Mum's behavior is too much. I sag against the wall. What I really want is to climb into my own bed, pull the Hello Kitty duvet over my head and sleep forever.

Then Mum says in a low voice, "Of course you're leaving. I always knew you would as soon as you turned sixteen. That's what I told the boy."

"What boy?"

"He was here yesterday, banging on the door, saying you wouldn't answer your phone. I didn't let him in."

Jordan? I think, but I'm so tired and confused, I just feel numb. That's all over, Josie, I tell myself. Anyway, maybe it was just Dom with news of Tasha. After all, Mum doesn't know any of these people. She doesn't know Mel or Ivy or Len, or people like the Princes with their wonderful house and perfect lives. My mum lives in this insane bubble, and all she's got is me.

I look at her standing in front of me, literally shaking, green eyes wide with terror, her awful prison haircut sticking out of her scalp. She thinks I'm about to walk away from her forever, and yes, I admit it. Part of me would love to do just that.

But I can't, can I? She looks so, well, helpless.

I have my principles too, and this is my mum. I can't abandon her.

I give a sigh and say, "Nice cup of tea?"

Mum wipes her eyes on her sleeve and nods.

We go up to my bedroom, which is still clean and tidy, and I put on the kettle.

Mum sits on my bed, stroking the Hello Kitty duvet. "It's nice in here."

"This is how the whole house should be, Mum."

She's silent for ages and ages. I make the tea and put her cup down on the bedside table. She sips it and I sit at my desk and stare at Tasha's laptop. I suppose I should ring her, arrange to give it back.

My phone's on my bedside table, and I pick it up. Loads of missed calls and text messages from Mum, Dom and Jordan. I don't have the energy to start going through them.

"Who did you stay with last night?" Mum says suddenly.

"I slept on the streets."

"Josie! God, no! I can't believe it." She grabs my arm and grips it so tight it hurts. "Why didn't you come home? God! Anything could have happened to you." Tears are pouring down her cheeks again.

"You know why I didn't come home, Mum, and you know

I don't have any friends to sleepover with, because..." I sweep my hand toward the mound of stuff still piled against the wall. "Because I live with a hoarder."

Mum gasps and let's go of my arm. Her head drops almost to her chest.

She's silent again for ages.

I start thinking about telling her to leave so I can go to bed, but then she says, "When I was in prison, I wasn't very well. They sent me to the psychiatrist and he gave me some pills to calm me down. I think they made me a bit dopy."

"Not sure about the haircut," I say cautiously.

She runs her hand through the short spikes. "Horrible, isn't it? One of the girls did it. Shirl egged her on. Wasn't much I could do. They're all very scary in there."

I feel a surge of anger and snap, "Why did you send Shirl and Bazza here?"

"I couldn't think straight in prison. I was scared and homesick, missing you and..."

"The hoard," I growl.

She flinches.

I keep my eyes fixed on my phone, so she carries on, "Shirl was kind. I think she sort of got me under her influence, what with the pills and being doped up, so I gave her the letter for you."

"Which she read and showed to that monster, Bazza! Didn't it occur to you that she might come around and rob us?"

Mum shook her head, her eyes wide with fear and shame.

"Why didn't you ring me, Mum? I waited and waited, but I heard nothing from you."

"I couldn't, the girls all listen to your phone calls. There's nowhere private in prison. I just thought once you read the letter, you'd write back."

I give a huge impatient sigh. How dumb is that!

But she looks so sad and hopeless, her shoulders slumped, gripping her mug like Tasha grips Mickey Mouse for comfort. I can't yell at her again.

We're quiet for a bit, and then she says in a tiny voice, "The psychiatrist told me I'm an obsessive-compulsive hoarder, and I need help or I'm going to lose you."

"I know, Mum."

"So why didn't you tell me?"

"You wouldn't have listened. Anyway, I only just realized it."

Both of us are very tired for the rest of Saturday. We sleep on and off for hours, and then around six, Mum orders Chinese takeaway.

"We're not eating that in the bedroom," I say when it arrives.

"But—"

"No, Mum! It makes the room smell. We can sit on the stairs."

She opens her mouth to argue again and then she snaps it shut and nods.

After we finish I collect all the cartons and take them out to the bin in the side passage. When I come back, Mum's sitting on her hands, shaking and rocking her body from side to side.

"Mum, listen," I say, grabbing her by the shoulders. She looks up at me. "We can start proper recycling once the house is clear and clean. I do believe in saving the planet."

"You do?"

"Sure. There's no other way to stop climate change and all that. But we can't do it all by ourselves, can we?"

"That's what the psychiatrist said. He said that if I don't clear the hoard and make our house a nice place for you to bring your friends over, then I'll lose you." Her voice drops to a whisper. "You're sixteen now, so I'll be all alone again."

"No, Mum! You won't! There's nothing magic about being sixteen. I'm not going to disappear."

"But look what happened when I turned sixteen."

"I'm not you. I'm Josie Tate, and I want to live with my lovely mum with her strong principles, and we're going to save the planet together. Only no more secondhand shops, right?"

"I'll try, Josie, I promise."

By nine we're both ready for bed, and when I kiss Mum goodnight at her bedroom door, it feels so good. I really did miss her. Now I know how much she loves me. She's agreed to let me ask the Russian brothers if they will come back and empty the house, and then they can put in a new bathroom. This time we're going to pay them properly from Grandpa's money.

I can't wait.

I fall asleep as soon as my head touches my lovely clean pillow, and then I'm woken by a thundering sound on the front door. Sunlight's pouring through the window, and my bedside clock says eleven thirty. I've slept for over twelve hours.

My bedroom door opens, and Mum puts her head around. "Don't answer," she says, her eyebrows furrowed.

No way, I think. I get up, pull a sweater over my pajamas and say, "Mum, things are different now. When someone comes to the door, we open it."

She walks off to her own room, muttering to herself, but she doesn't try to stop me.

Progress, I tell myself, as the thundering on the door

gets louder. My phone's bleeping too, so I pick it up and go downstairs.

I open the door, and there's Jordan. He reaches out to grab me, but I push the door half shut. I'm not ready for this, not after the way he stormed off on Friday.

"Josie," he says. "Come on, give me a hug. Where've you been? I've been so worried. Your mom wouldn't open the door or tell me anything."

"Sure," I say.

He stares down at me, a confused look on his face, then he says, "I know you're mad at me. I get it—honest, I do. I ran off. Again."

"That's about right," I say in a cool voice.

He shrugs and taps his arm. "Hey, look—no damage, just a bruise. I've been training for hours this morning. I'm still on the team heading for the Olympics."

"That's all right then," and I give a bit of snort, like Tasha would. Or Mocha.

His almond eyes retreat into their sockets, and he says in a low voice, "So how about us?"

I stare at him for almost a minute, but he drops his head, can't meet my eyes.

Then I take a deep breath and say, "My mum is an obsessive-compulsive hoarder, and my house needs sorting out from top to bottom. We don't live like you, Jordan, but if you still want to be my boyfriend, then you have to accept me the way I am."

His eyes widen and he nods, saying, "Sure, Josie, I get it. But I've seen those hoarder programs on TV. Do you really think she can change?"

"She knows I'll move out if she doesn't."

"Okay, so . . . move in with us. Plenty of room."

"Jordan Prince! Are you asking me to live with you?"

He ducks his head again and then he looks back up at me, still grinning, and says, "Hey, why not? Or we could go for a burger and a shake."

I feel that familiar flutter in my heart, and I have to admit that even though Jordan's life is wrapped in cotton wool, he keeps coming back, no matter what he finds out about me and my life. I can't let him go, can I? But I have to be sure.

"Even though my mum's a hoarder and my house is disgusting?"

"I don't care. You're my girlfriend, and I want to be with you."

"Right answer, boyfriend."

Jordan leans forward until our foreheads are touching, and then I turn my face and we kiss. It feels just the same, just like it was before Mum came home and tried to spoil my life again. But I'm turning our lives around. I've taken charge, and she's realized she has to change. We're starting a new life together.

I know I want Jordan to be a part of that life.

I'm just about to peel away so I can get ready to go out when my phone rings. It's Dom.

"Josie! You have to come. Tasha's collapsed—she's in the hospital." He clicks off before I can speak.

"What's up?" says Jordan.

"Tasha's in the hospital. I have to go."

"I'll call a cab," he says, already punching his phone. "Go and get dressed. It'll be quicker."

I hesitate, and then I say, "Okay."

As I run upstairs, calling to Mum and then getting dressed, I hope I've made the right decision about Jordan. Only time will tell. But right now, we have to sort out Tasha Brown.

34. Tasha

Thursday night my phone goes. It's Dom. Since he found me in the hospital on Sunday, he rings every couple of hours. He hasn't said any more about going out with Freckly Emily. Maybe it didn't work out. Who cares?

"Fireworks this weekend," he says.

"So?"

The children's home is having a party for the eleven-year-old twins who never speak and for Stefan who's twelve and in a wheelchair. They've already said no sparklers—health and safety—and everyone has to watch through the patio doors in the living room.

Totally lame.

"Clay, my cousin, is having a party Saturday night with booze, barbecue, fireworks and a spinning-wheel firework setup the size of the London Eye," says Dom.

"Always wanted to go on the London Eye," I say, feeling miserable.

"That can be arranged. Anyhow, pick you up at eight."

His voice sounds so normal. He has no idea. I'm in care now; I don't live with normal parents in a normal home and go to normal parties.

"Tash?"

"My social worker won't let me."

"Yes, she will. I've fixed it."

"What?"

"Got my mum to ring the home. We've promised my dad will drive us to and from, and you'll be back by eleven."

"No way."

"Way, babes! Who's the legend?"

I can't help laughing, my sweet little Dom trying to be cool. He'll never get there, but so what?

"Dominique Steven Jensen, *you* are a total legend."

Tasha's Vlog
Thursday, October 31, 9:56 p.m.
I've been at Acorns Children's Home since Tuesday. It's horrible like I always knew it would be. Just look at the wallpaper.

Camera pans bedroom.

At least I don't have to share. Yet. Jen, my key worker—*groan*—says if another girl arrives, she'll have to go in with me. I wish Josie was here. We had so much fun squeezed into her stupid bed. I asked her on Sunday when she came to see me in hospital with Jordan, if she'd kept the Hello Kitty duvet. 'Course, she said, reminds me of your toenails digging into me.

Dom came later after the others had gone. I stared and stared at him while he talked away about school and stuff. Then he said, I better go, meeting Emily to study. He leaned over and kissed me on the cheek before he disappeared.

I knew then for certain that Josie and Jordan had been right. Dom had fallen in love with me—not sure when, but definitely in the past few months. But I couldn't see it. It's like I missed that bit of him—overlooked it, didn't bother to pay attention—and now it's too late. Dom has given up on me and fallen for geeky Emily.

I'm all alone again. I cry a lot these days and the social worker says it's the concussion. But it's not. It's because I didn't realize I was in love with Dom. Crazy, stupid me.

Pause.

I'm crying so much I can't go on with the vlog. I still don't feel very well. They said in the hospital that I had a delayed concussion and a fever because of an infection. So I have to take about a million pills.

The social workers were called in. I told them about Chaz and said I didn't want to go home. So I ended up in a children's home. Mum has to come to some sort of stupid meeting next week to explain. Whatever she says, I don't want to live with her anymore. The social workers said I don't have to if I don't feel safe.

Bottom line, I don't trust her, and she's said nothing about kicking Chaz out. She hasn't even texted me or been to visit me or anything. So I'm stuck in Acorns until I leave school and get my own flat. Just like Josie wanted. Only *she* doesn't need one anymore.

I was right about Mum, wasn't I? Even when I end up in the hospital, she doesn't change. My mum doesn't love me or care about me, not like Josie's mum. Sounds like prison was just what *she* needed, because it's all hunky-dory in the hoarder house these days.

I can't go to school until next week, and it's so boring hanging around the home all day. At least Josie brought my laptop to the hospital. Dom says she and Jordan will be at the party, but what's the point? I haven't even got anything to wear.

Saturday morning, Jen takes me out to buy a new outfit. "Got to look good for your hot date," she says, grinning.

"Dom's not my boyfriend," I mutter.

She gives me a curious look. She's older than Mum, almost ancient, so what does she know?

But we get skinny black jeans and a really nice jacket that ends at my waist and has a sparkly stripe down each sleeve. As I stare in the mirror, I can't help wishing Rory would be there tonight and fall in love with me.

"No one loves you, Tasha Brown," I whisper.

People who work in a children's home do it for the money. They don't really care what happens to you. That's what mums and dads and brothers and sisters are supposed to do, like they do in Dom's family. I don't have any of those anymore. I don't have a home. I have a care home. It's not the same no matter what they try to do, calling it Acorns as if it's a country mansion with pictures on the wall and matching mugs and plates in the kitchen. The other kids are nothing to me. I wouldn't care if they all disappeared.

I go out of the changing room and show Jen. "That looks really nice, Tasha. Will you be warm enough, sweetheart?"

She has a concerned look on her face, but it's all a pose, isn't it? I shrug. "Who cares?"

"I do," says Jen in a quiet voice.

I feel a bit mean, so I say, "I could take a scarf."

"Lovely, let's get one now to match."

We choose a gray woolly scarf and Jen winds it around my neck, saying, "You look very cozy."

She wears a light perfume, which I like, and her hands winding the scarf around me are gentle. Something inside me softens, and I say, "Thanks, Jen."

"You're welcome, sweetheart. Much better you go off to a party with your friends than hang around Acorns with the little ones."

Tasha's Vlog
Saturday, Nov. 2, 4:45 p.m.
It was nice going shopping today, just me and Jen. She's okay, I suppose. At least she doesn't treat me like a kid. Mostly, I like it that they leave me alone in here. I'm supposed to rest a lot to get over my bad head, and it's quiet in my room. The other kids like to sit downstairs with the social workers and play stupid games.

I've been surfing the Internet. They have great wifi in the home. On YouTube there's loads of teens like me making vlogs, and I've got all these friends now. They're all over the world, and some of them live in children's homes. It's like having a whole new crowd to hang out with, only I don't have to leave the house.

#Konrad2491 from Hamburg put up a vlog yesterday about ending up on the streets after his stepdad threw him out. He's only twelve.

He says it's much better in a children's home. "I feel happy, safer and no drugs," he said on his vlog. His face has a big scar down one cheek. I wonder who did that?

I put up a comment about the firework party tonight.

Konrad commented back that I should tell them about it tomorrow.

We'll see. Only if something interesting happens.

Bored yawn.

Saturday night Dom is pressing the doorbell dead on eight. Jen calls out to me, "Have a lovely time, sweetheart."

I give her a smile, swing my scarf around my neck and go out the door. I feel as though I've been released from a cage.

"Where's Emily?" I say, expecting her to be in the car too.

Dom knits his eyebrows and says, "She's not coming."

We settle down in the backseat together. His thigh is touching mine, and it feels so warm and friendly. His fresh sweet scent wafts over me.

I'm desperate for this evening to go really well after being so miserable and lonely the past few weeks. Even Josie's life with her crazy mum has worked out. All mine wants to do is slap me in the face.

So I say, "Thanks, Dom."

He raises an eyebrow, and he's staring into my eyes.

"You know," I say, "for sticking by me through all this crazy stuff about Chaz and my mum and me going into care."

"It's nothing, Tasha. You mean the world to me."

He puts out the pinky on his left hand, like he used to do in school when we were babies and someone was being horrible to me. Chocolate and cream, we used to call his dark brown finger with my white one. I link the pinky on my right hand, and we stay like that until we get to the party. I wish we could stay like this forever.

Dom's cousin, Clay, is really tall and a couple of years older than us. He and Dom fool around fist bumping for a bit, and then he hands us soft drinks—I'm not allowed alcohol with my concussion—and wanders off. The garden's packed with Clay's friends from college and loads of Dom's cousins. He has a really huge family.

Someone taps me on a shoulder, and I turn to see Josie grinning, Jordan's arm draped around her.

"Yaay! Tasha Brown," says Josie, and she gives me a hug.

Jordan pats my arm, and they stand there by the light of the fire. Josie has a lovely necklace with a gold heart glinting around her neck.

"Present?" I say.

"Jordan gave it to me for my birthday."

"Nice."

"It's good to see you and Dom," she says.

Dom comes up with hot dogs, and Jordan drags Josie off to get some too. Rockets are screaming into the night sky, and the fire's lighting up all the happy faces.

Then Clay lights the spinning wheel, and Dom was right: it's the biggest firework I've ever seen. The bonfire's really hot now.

As I stare at the whirling wheel of fire, mesmerized by the light, Dom pulls me gently back. Its cooler in the shadows. The light from the wheel is spinning like a crazy weird sun. I want it to go on forever so that I don't have to come back to reality and the life that has been dished up for me, the life I would never have chosen.

Dom calls out to his cousin on the other side of the bonfire, "All right, Clay? Random party, man."

He's standing right behind me. I can almost feel the heat from his body through my jacket.

The fireworks have finished, and I turn to face Dom. For the first time, I realize that his eyes are level with mine. My sweet little Dom has grown this autumn, and his voice has finally broken too. How did I miss all this? I was so full of my own misery that I ignored him, practically pushed him into Emily's arms.

But she isn't here tonight.

Is this my moment? I wonder. If I don't act now, take it and grab it and love it, then maybe my chance will disappear forever like the fireworks.

I close my eyes, lean forward and kiss Dom on the lips. For a second there's nothing, and I nearly pull back as a stab of disappointment plunges through me.

Then he kisses me back, and it's the sweetest moment in my whole life.

We kiss and kiss until we run out of breath.

He pulls back, staring into my eyes, and says, "So are we cool, Tish Tash?"

His voice is so gentle and yet so certain. He knows he wants this.

"We're cool," I say.

Then he puts his arms around me, and as I rest my cheek on his shoulder, I know that finally I have come home.

About Miriam Halahmy

Miriam Halahmy has published novels, short stories, and poetry for adults and young people. Her stories and poems have been included in anthologies, read on the radio, performed on stage and set to music. Her novels are built around strong characters and real-life situations. Miriam believes that teen-age hopes, fears, dreams and, above all, relationships should be respected by everyone.

Miriam lives in London and is married with two grown-up children. When she is not writing, she enjoys painting, travel-ing, visiting her favorite seaside place and spending time with her family. Miriam continues to work on novels for young peo-ple and enjoys meeting her audiences in schools, colleges and at book festivals around the UK and Europe.

A Note from the Author

I would like to thank my trusted readers and supportive fellow writers who have commented on drafts of this book. A special thanks to Caroline Hooton for legal advice in relation to the nonpayment of council tax.

Rhys Gormley, Head Coach of the Barnet Copthall Swimming Club, gave invaluable information about the training of future Olympic swimmers.

When I was a teenager, a film by the director Ken Loach called *Cathy Come Home* was shown on British television. The film is a heartrending story about a young couple with children who fall on hard times and eventually become homeless. It sparked my lifelong interest in the plight of homeless people.

According to the Joseph Rowntree Foundation (www.jrf.org.uk), at least 75,000 young people are in contact with homeless services each year. More young women than young men are likely to end up homeless. The main trigger for youth homelessness is relationship breakdown.

For different reasons, my characters, Josie and Tasha, are faced with a life on the streets that would put them at risk for abuse, addiction, crime and disease.

We still have a great deal to do in our society to make sure that no one sleeps rough on our streets.

Miriam Halahmy
www.miriamhalahmy.com